MW01204964

Walk Past the Wolf

Walk Past the Wolf

A Mythmatical Battles Adventure

by
Scrivener Minion

4R, Inc.

For Nick

Chapter 1

Nick Snow had never seen it. That was about to change.

Nick didn't know that of course. As he trudged home from school under the hot Florida sun, Nick wasn't thinking of snow. And he certainly didn't suspect he was about to have an Adventure where he'd see more snow than he'd ever want, along with an eight-legged horse and whispering crows and angry giants and, well, quite a few other things that we'll get to a little later. Let's just say that, in spite of his name, young Mr. Snow didn't have the slightest clue that a snow-filled adventure was barreling right at him.

But it was coming just the same.

For now though, Nick was as far away from snow as you could imagine. On this sunny, muggy Florida afternoon, Nick was walking home from school with his friend Chris. Actually, walking isn't the right word. Nick was shuffling along the sidewalk, head down, leaning forward against the weight of the fully stuffed backpack hanging from his shoulders. Despite the heat, he wore a long-sleeved, gray t-shirt that drooped from his thin shoulders and dark jeans. Every few steps, he hitched up those jeans in a never-ending battle to keep the pants from slipping down off his narrow waist and adjusted his straps to keep the backpack from sliding off his shoulders.

Most days, Nick did this without thinking as he and Chris talked and laughed all the way home. Not on this day though. Today, Nick wasn't talking and he certainly wasn't laughing. Today, Nick was just walking, head down, dragging his skateboard next to him, the only sound the methodical, regular clack of its back two wheels hitting the seams in the sidewalk.

Now Nick's head wasn't down because of his backpack, which was always this heavy. And he wasn't sweating because it was hot, although it certainly was hot that day. No, Nick's head was down because he was embarassed. And sweat was running down the back of his neck because he believed he was dead. Very, very dead.

"I'm dead," said Nick.

"Why didn't you just go up there, Nick?" asked Chris.

"I didn't know the answer," Nick replied.

"You knew it," said Chris. "We did it last night. You said all the 7's three times!"

"Yeah but if I did the 7's, I'd have to do the 8's."

"So you'd do the 8's!"

"I can't remember the 8's," said Nick quietly.

"You can, Nick. We studied them for an hour last night."

"I can't count by 8's," repeated Nick.

"Okay," agreed Chris reluctantly. "But why the heck did you say that to Mr. Fredrickson?"

Nick shrugged, head still down. As hot as he was, it was nothing compared to the heat he'd felt in his face when Mr. Fredrickson had told him to come to the front of the class for his turn at the blackboard during the math relay. Nick had been scared enough that he wouldn't know his 8's. But walking up in front of the class, past all those kids, with all those eyes focused on him, just him, as he struggled to do the problem on the board? No way. He hadn't been able to move.

Mr. Fredrickson was about as good a sixth grade teacher as you could find and Nick knew that if he'd just told Mr. Fredrickson that he was scared and didn't want to go up in front of the class, he probably would have skipped Nick and moved on to the next kid. But instead, when Mr. Frederickson had said "Nick, your turn, go up to the board," Nick had looked up at the six foot four teacher and said the first thing that popped into his head:

"Make me."

Fortunately for Nick, the good-natured Mr. Frederickson decided not to squish him. Instead, he sent Nick straight to the principal's office.

Giving his dad the test in his backpack was going to be bad enough. The detention slip, though. . . . More sweat poured down the side of Nick's face. How was he going to explain he'd just been scared, that he'd panicked? He knew that would never excuse the rudeness of what he'd said. At least not to his father.

Nick sighed again. "Dad is going to kill me."

"Don't worry," said Chris. "Your Dad'll understand about the test. It's not like he's a rocket scientist or something. Oh yeah," Chris grinned. "He is."

Nick actually groaned at the reminder as he hitched up his jeans again. The trickle of sweat grew to a small stream. Nick's dad rarely raised his voice to Nick so he and Chris were exaggerating. A little. But the fiery rays of the Florida sun burning the back of Nick's neck still felt cooler than the glare Nick was expecting when he got home.

"Wanna come over to my house first?" Chris asked. "We can game until your dad gets home."

Nick thought for a minute, wanting to take the chance but unsure if he could. "No," he said finally. "Mom said I have to come straight home so we can get ready go to Clearwater for the weekend to visit my grandma."

"Too bad. Probably the last time you'll get to play for awhile."

"Got that right."

They stopped at Nick's driveway. The afternoon heat radiated up from the pavement at Nick's feet. Funny how he usually didn't notice it.

"I'll see you tomorrow, Chris. If I'm still alive."

"Ah, I'm sure he won't care Nick."

"Yeah?" replied Nick hopefully.

"Yeah. Hey look!" yelled Chris and pointed up at the sky. "A flying pig!"

"Yeah," said Nick, his hope dying. "Thanks."

Chris gave him a cheerful wave. "Nice knowin' ya, Nick." Chris put his headphones on and hummed his way down the street.

Nick turned and started up the walk to his house, barely noticing the sun, the plants, and the darn birds whose happy chirping would fool anyone into thinking that the world wasn't going to end today. They obviously didn't have to take math tests. And they obviously didn't have to explain to their father, their ROCKET SCIENTIST FATHER, that they'd just gotten their fourth D in a row.

He pressed 1−1−0−3 on the garage door key pad. His heart sank as he saw the tires, then the bumper, then the rear window of his father's Jeep.

Nick's dad was already home. He wasn't even going to get to play a farewell game.

★ ★ ★

James Snow was an altogether imposing man. Tall, straight, and serious, he had a way of wearing a dark three button shirt and sharply pressed khakis like a military uniform. Even as he stood at their kitchen's island, flipping through bills, he looked every inch like one of the first African-Americans to be launched into space. Nick had a sinking feeling he was next.

"Son," he rumbled with a smile.

"Hi, Dad." Nick gambled on the direct approach (an excellent tactic in both military and parental maneuvers). He walked right up to his dad and hugged him, still holding his skateboard in one hand. Then, the moment his dad's grip loosened, he walked straight toward his room.

"Son?"

Nick stopped, still facing the hallway. "Yeah?"

"How was school?"

"Good."

"Lunch?"

"Good. Pizza."

"Skateboards at recess?"

"No. Andy Swy broke his arm last week. They're making us play kickball now instead."

"Hmmm." His dad started leafing through the bills again. Nick took that as a sign to bolt. He headed for the hallway and freedom.

"Son."

Nick froze.

"How was the math test?"

New sweat trickled down Nick's neck as he turned. "Fine."

James Snow stared at Nick with eyes that had surveyed the Earth from space. Nick felt just as small.

"Did you get it back yet?"

Excuses jumped through Nick's head like rabbits. Mr. Frederickson didn't give them back yet. Mr. Frederickson had a heart attack. The school was attacked by a swarm of test termites. The State turned our school into a clown college so there's no more math. The CIA seized all the tests for national security reasons.

Nick didn't even buy them. That left only one terrible option.

"Yes, Dad."

"Let's see it."

Nick rummaged around in his backpack, head down. By the time he pulled out the test, his stomach was fluttering like its pages.

James Snow took it, those eyes boring into the big red "61%" at the top of the page. Nick started the countdown and waited for blast-off. 10–9–8–7–6–5–4–3–2–1. . . .

Instead of exploding, James Snow looked at Nick with a face which was serious, but calm. "Did you try your best Nick?"

"Yes, Dad."

"Study with Chris last night?"

"Yes, Dad."

James Snow glanced at the test again before he set it down on the island. "Still having trouble with 8's?"

Nick face felt hot as his eyes stayed on the big red "61." "Yes, Dad."

"Is there something else you wanted to tell me?"

Nick started, caught completely off-guard by his dad's question. How could he have known about the detention? He couldn't have known about the detention. Could he?

Nick stared at his dad, unable to make his mouth work. James Snow stared calmly back. "I got a call from Mr. Frederickson today."

When his dad paused again, Nick knew that blast-off must be coming now. Nice knowin' you Chris, he thought. I'll play with you again when I'm 30.

"He said you were pretty nervous about getting up in front of the class today to do your multiplication. Is that true?"

Nick's mouth was half open with an excuse for why he hadn't meant to say what he did to Mr. Frederickson when he stopped and closed it again. His dad wasn't talking about detention. And Nick hadn't told Mr. Frederickson that he'd been scared.

"Were you scared to get up in front of the class, Son?"

Nick felt embarrassed all over again. He looked down at the island and nodded.

"What do I tell you, Son?"

"Face your fear or it'll chase you forever," Nick said automatically. Easy to say when you've piloted a rocket ship. Nick figured a lecture was coming.

But on this day of surprises, Nick was wrong again. Without saying a word, James Snow reached into a bag on the counter and pulled out a small yellow box.

"What's this?" asked Nick.

"Something that will help. I hope."

Nick watched in amazement as his dad's mouth twitched. Was that a smile?

Nick took the box and looked at this golden Get Out of Jail Key. The box had a shield on the front, half black and half red. A gold M and B were combined on the face of the shield. To the left of the shield was a picture of a blond man swinging a hammer. On the right, a bird-headed man stood below a floating eye. "Mythmatical Battles," Nick read aloud. "Norse and Egyptian?"

"One deck of each," said James Snow. "It's a multiplication game. I thought we'd play on vacation."

Nick stared, as intrigued by the box as he was amazed that he was not grounded. He opened the top of the box and read the curious scroll on it—"*The Adventure Card is the Key. Brace yourself.*" He shook two sealed decks onto the counter and reached for the gold and yellow one that said "Egyptian" on the back of the top card. He ripped open the cellophane and began leafing through the cards. "Isis. The Ferryman. Cobra. Geezow, look at all these Dad!" He shuffled through some more until he came to one and held it up. "Look, Ramses the Second."

James Snow nodded. "Like at the museum exhibit last year."

"How do you play?" Nick asked.

"I think you use these two multiplication equations on the bottom of each card." James Snow stared at the cards for a moment and then at the directions he had unfolded. He handed the directions to Nick. "Why don't you take this back to your room and figure it out. You can show me how to play when we get to your grandma's."

"Okay." Nick collected the cards, directions, and box and started to his room.

"Son," he was halted again.

"Yes, Dad?"

James Snow held up the test. "This will come up. When it does, the fear will go down. We'll work on it together."

"Thanks, Dad," Nick grinned, and sprinted down the hall.

Nick felt lighter. The heat of his fear cooled and he felt a rush of relief as he realized that he wasn't grounded, he wasn't getting yelled at, and he wasn't dead. Instead, his dad had surprised him with a gift. And a game at that! As he opened the door to his room, Nick knew he couldn't have had a more unexpected ending to his day.

Boy was he wrong.

Chapter 2

Now to really understand how excited Nick was about this strange new card game, you have to know how Nick felt about Egypt. It had started the year before when Nick's dad had taken the whole family to a museum exhibit of ancient Egyptian artifacts. Nick remembered how excited his dad had been to see artifacts from the cradle of civilization but to Nick, the thought of spending an entire Saturday afternoon stuck in a museum had sounded as appetizing as peas.

But they'd started the day with a mummification workshop where Nick and his younger brother had made their own (fake) mummy, complete with jars for the guts. Then, they went on a private tour of the exhibit and were allowed to sit on a 4000 year old stone lion and make pencil rubbings of a hieroglyphics tablet. By the time they saw the highlight of the exhibit—two real, live (well, dead actually) mummies, one of them partially unwrapped—Nick had decided two things. First, having an astronaut dad was actually good for something. Second, he loved anything Egyptian. Movies, posters, toys, or books, it didn't matter. If it had Pyramids or Sphinxes or Pharaohs or Mummies or Scarabs or Crocs, Nick watched it or played it or read it.

So by the time Nick opened the door to his room and hopped onto his bed, he couldn't wait to check out this new

Egyptian deck from his dad. He flipped his skateboard at his pillow, hardly noticing as a bolt caught on his pillowcase and ripped the fabric. He paid no attention to the small puff of feathers that floated into the air but instead crossed his legs and began looking at what was in the Egyptian deck.

He laid the cards out in rows in front of him; gods and heroes on one side, monsters and minions on the other. The weapons and magic cards he piled in between. Already, he saw some of his favorite Egyptian legends and some new ones he was anxious to read.

Ready to really dig in, he picked up the first god card, a winged female named Ma'at, and read the description under the picture:

> *The cat-headed goddess presides over truth, justice, and harmony. The weight of her feather decides if one's heart is good or evil. She cannot be attacked by minions.*

He laid the Ma'at card back down and picked up the next one, Osiris.

A card slipped from behind Osiris and fell to the bed, face down. Unlike the rest of the gold Egyptian cards, this one was red with a tan background. And instead of "Egyptian," a different word was written in bright yellow above the MB shield: *Adventure.*

Nick scrunched his eyebrows together and turned the odd card over. There was nothing ancient or Egyptian about the picture. Instead, it showed a modern girl about his age in jeans with long black hair. A puppy faced her as she sat cross-legged, holding a turtle of all things. Her inscription was different too:

> *Bella Reddy knew a lot about animals.*
> *But not the kind she was about to meet.*

And then that line again:

The Adventure card is the Key. Brace yourself.

Nick turned the Adventure card over again, staring. He pushed his other cards around, looking for more like it in the Egyptian deck. There weren't any. He held the card for a moment, uncertain what to do with it. Probably a wild card or something, he thought. He shrugged, decided to figure it out later, and set the Adventure card aside.

Nick spent the next hour reading each of the cards. He first worked through the gods (he preferred Seth), before he moved to the heroes (Ramses was still the favorite there), and then the monsters (he actually crowed when he saw the Phoenix), and finally the minions (where he ended with the Seven Scorpions of Isis). Next, he leafed through the weapons cards which were an assortment of wands, staffs, and even feathers. Then he finished with the series of mysterious Egyptian books, amulets, and events shown on the magic cards.

Nick's excitement grew with each card. He couldn't believe his luck. Playing this game was going to beat the pants off of studying flashcards. By the time he was done, he couldn't wait to show his dad.

"Nick," came his mom's voice from down the hall. "Start getting your stuff together. We're leaving in half an hour."

"Okay, Mom," Nick called back. He gathered the Egyptian deck into a neat pile, being careful to keep the cards in order, and put them back in the box. Then he folded the directions and tried to stuff them back into the box with the cards but, no matter how much he pushed, they kept catching on the inside. Frustrated, he finally shook everything out of the box onto his bed to start over.

The directions, a sheet called "The Legend," and the loose Egyptian cards scattered across his sheets. The last thing to slide out was a blue card deck, still wrapped in its plastic. Nick picked it up and studied the ice blue card back of the Norse deck, which looked as cold as the Egyptian cards looked hot.

Nick didn't know anything about Norse legends. He'd heard of Thor of course (he may have had trouble with math but he wasn't stupid). He thought they had something to do with the Vikings but he wasn't sure. You see, Nick had lived in Florida his whole life and, as a state, Florida was decidedly short on Norsemen. In fact, Nick had never even seen snow.

He glanced at the hallway, didn't see his mom standing there, and decided to take a quick peek at the blue Norse deck to see if it had any cool cards. He ripped open the plastic wrap and tossed it. He quickly flipped the cards over, anxious to see the Norse gods and monsters he'd be using to battle his Egyptian deck.

The first card had nothing on it—no picture, no name, no equations, nothing. The same was true of the second. And the third. And the fourth. Nick shuffled through the deck quicker. He saw one light blue rectangle after another.

They were all blank.

"What a rip!" Nick said, flipping the cards back and forth. Not a single one of these blue cards had anything printed on them. Figures, he thought. My dad gives me a game that gets me out of studying and it's broken. Or whatever you call not printing cards.

"N-i-i-i-ck. You getting ready?" His mom again.

"Yes, Mom." Disgusted, Nick put the blank Norse deck together and started to push it into the box along with the Egyptian deck. As he did, he saw a flash of red in the middle of the blue card backs. He pulled the deck back out and quickly rifled through it until he came to the red card. It was another Adventure card. Nick pulled out the card and flipped it over.

He froze.

The upper right corner of the card said "Adventure." Below it was the picture of an African-American boy wearing a long-sleeved gray shirt and baggy jeans. The clothes hung loosely, as if the boy were thin. The boy was standing on a skateboard and held an MP3 player. Nick didn't have to look to know the boy's name but his eyes were drawn to the upper left corner of the card anyway.

It said "Nick Snow."

Even after he read it, he didn't believe it. Nick blinked his eyes and shivered as a chill crept along the back of his neck. A couple of the feathers from his pillow swirled up to his nose. He couldn't tear his eyes away from the card.

With excitement and dread, he read the inscription under the picture:

Nick Snow had never seen it. That was about to change.

The Adventure card is the key. Brace yourself.

As he finished reading, Nick heard the blast of a horn, a single piercing note that was far off, at the edge of his hearing. At the same time, a stream of feathers burst straight up from his pillow like a geyser. The cool breeze at Nick's back became an icy gale which caught the feathers and swirled them around Nick's head until all he saw was a blur of white.

"Dad!" Nick screamed. "Daaaaaaaaddddddd!" But Nick could barely hear his own voice in the new roar of the swirling wind. The horn rang out again. Louder this time. And closer.

Nick was too young to question his sanity but he knew freaky when he saw it. He jumped from his bed and lurched for the door, unable to see it in the driving white feather storm. He tripped over something and fell face first into a mound of cold feathers. The horn sounded a third time, so close it shook his spine.

Nick raised his face from the pile and wiped the feathers from his eyes with the back of his arm. They were wet and stuck to his cheeks. Blinking furiously, he scrambled to his feet and slid toward where his door should be. He slipped to his knees, catching himself in another pile of feathers.

The whirlwind abruptly dropped and the feathers slowed their blinding flight until Nick was surrounded by a steady fall of gently drifting white. Except, as you've probably already figured out, it wasn't feathers. He held out his hand, caught a feather, and watched it melt into a drop of water.

It was snow. Gently falling snow. The feathers were all gone. So was his room.

Nick stood and stepped forward to where his door should have been. Instead of the smooth white panel of his door, he reached out and placed his hand on the trunk of an enormous tree. He rubbed the trunk in disbelief until the cold edges of the rough bark bit at his hand.

He looked around and saw, not the walls of his room, but tree after towering tree. He was standing on the edge of a forest. (A forest!) Before this really sank in, the horn blasted for a fourth time, seemingly right behind him. Startled, Nick jumped to the other side of the tree, farther into the strange woods.

Which was fortunate. For at that moment, a giant crashed out of the trees.

*

Chapter 3

As the giant snarled into the open, Nick dove behind a tree (something you should do if a giant ever crashes out of a woods near you). Nick hit a snowdrift face first and burrowed into it as deeply as he could, pressing himself down under snow and against wood, hoping the giant would pass him without noticing. He scrunched down a little farther just to be safe and then, little by little, peeked around the trunk.

The giant was big and blue and bald. He was so tall Nick thought he could look down on a basketball rim. His massive blue arms bulged out of a sleeveless leather tunic as he whipped a blue flag and a sword back and forth over his head. The giant opened a mouth filled with snaggled yellow teeth and bellowed. Nick shook, suddenly certain that this was not a "jolly" green giant. This was an "I'm going to eat you" blue one.

Nick ducked his head, both confused and afraid. Just a minute ago he'd been trying to avoid a grounding for a math grade and now he was trying to avoid being ground up by snaggly giant teeth. The giant bellowed again and Nick burrowed deeper, concentrating completely on not becoming a Nick Nugget.

A horn echoed in answer to the giant's roar. A second later, a pack of huge, rangy dogs tumbled out of the woods, leaping one after the other over the trees the giant had broken.

The giant stepped back, swinging his sword and flag as the pack of shaggy wolfhounds hit him. The gray fur and blue skin whirled so fast that Nick could barely see it (although he later admitted that his view was blocked as much by his fingers as by the flying snow). Nick heard a whelp and a howl, a crunch and a crack. When he looked again, five dogs lay dead in the snow. A sixth was limping back into the woods, whimpering. The giant bellowed again and flung his flag like a spear. There was a high-pitched screech, and then a horrible silence.

Nick wanted to puke. But instead he locked his eyes on the giant.

The blue giant stood alone in the clearing, breathing hard. White smoke billowed from his mouth with each breath and then slowly disappeared as it rose. (Now before you shout "It's his breath, stupid!" remember that Nick Snow had never seen it and that this was the first time he'd ever been in cold weather. Given the circumstances of his introduction, I think you can at least give him a moment to figure it out.) The giant raised his arms, tilted his head to the sky, and roared. Nick clapped his hands to his ears and pushed his head forward into the snow against the horrible sound.

The roar abruptly stopped. Nick waited a moment, then dropped his hands from his ears to check. He heard nothing. Slowly, he lifted his head from the snow and peeked around the trunk to look at the giant again.

The giant was looking back.

Nick froze. He didn't even breathe. The giant tilted his head with the same expression his dog Joe made when Nick gave him too many commands at once. The giant took a step forward. Then another, staring in Nick's direction the whole time. Nick didn't move. Since Nick had never been stared at by a dog-flinging giant before, he didn't know if sitting still was the right thing to do. But his legs were so numb with cold and his mind was so numb with fear that he wasn't sure if he'd have been able to run anyway.

No more than fifty feet away, the giant bent over, rested his hands on his knees, and stared straight at Nick's tree trunk. The giant took another step and hit a fur pile with his foot. He snorted, sending another puff of evaporating smoke out his nose, and looked down at the offending pile. He rummaged around with one hand and came up with a studded leather collar. The giant guffawed and tossed the collar aside.

With the giant's attention distracted by the ex-dog, Nick started to pull back behind the tree. As soon as Nick moved, the giant whipped his head back around, his yellow eyes boring through Nick's tree. Nick froze, so scared that he forgot to breathe again. The giant didn't move. Neither did Nick. He just sat rock-still and prayed that the giant wouldn't see him.

A second horn echoed in the forest, far away. The giant's eyes twitched towards the sound. Nick exhaled.

A white cloud poured out of Nick's mouth.

The giant's yellow eyes widened and Nick blurted a word he wasn't supposed to know. The giant roared and Nick leapt to his feet. Then the giant charged and Nick sprinted into the woods (proving that his legs weren't so numb with cold nor his mind so numb with fear that he couldn't run for his life from a dog-flinging, yellow-toothed, bald, blue giant).

Nick wasn't the fastest runner at school but he was quick and thin and he used both of those things as the forest grew more dense. Nick dashed through bushes and under trees. He squeezed through a thin gap in a thorn bush and dodged through a virtual fence of birch trees. He leapt over a fallen tree trunk and ducked under a low pine branch at the same time. He heard another roar, followed by the crack of snapping trees. Although it was too close (way, way, way too close), Nick thought that the crunching of branches was getting fainter and that the roar sounded more like a "where in the blue blazes is he" than a roar of "there's my tasty treat."

Then again you can never be too far from a hungry giant so Nick ran as hard as he could, his heart pounding with fear as his legs pounded the snow. Nick churned over a small snow bank and slid down the far side, straight into another thorn bush. The thorns held him, grabbing at his arms and face with dozens of small sharp fingers. Nick tried to peel the branches off him without getting poked but they only seemed to sink deeper into his clothes.

Suddenly, the giant howled right behind him. A second later, Nick heard a crack like a gunshot as a pine tree snapped and fell toward him. In a burst of panic, Nick ripped free of the thorns (leaving behind some shirt and some skin) and stumbled out of the trees into a huge, football field–sized clearing.

Keeping his head down, Nick sprinted as hard as he could in the soft snow. When he reached the middle of the clearing, he looked up, searching for a way out on the other side. What he saw brought him to a sliding, skittering stop.

Another giant.

This giant was even bigger than the first. He had a long white beard, a horned helmet, and leaned on a monstrous axe. When he saw Nick, he started to laugh, a sound somehow worse than the other giant's roar. "There's our rabbit," the new giant chuckled.

It was too much for Nick. He didn't run, he didn't yell, he didn't even look around for another way out. He just dropped to the ground, exhausted, and eleven, and scared to death. He huddled into the snow with his hands over his head but he couldn't take his eyes off the new giant that flipped his axe onto his shoulder and crossed the field toward Nick.

The giant's heavy steps sent puffs of snow into the air, making it look like he was walking through shimmering smoke. He stopped right in front of Nick, sending a fine mist of ice crystals drifting into Nick's face, making it burn strangely. Nick couldn't see that the ice crystals had frozen on the streaks of the tears running down his cheeks.

The new giant squatted down in front of Nick, which still left him six feet over Nick's head. Behind a mass of gray beard and hair, his green eyes sparkled mischievously.

"Give them to me," said the giant.

Nick didn't move and he didn't speak. He just kept his hands on his head and stared at the giant.

"Give them to me now, rabbit," the giant repeated and held out a hand as big as a basketball.

Nick just sat there, frozen. Now for those of you who are wondering, it doesn't pay to ignore a giant. But Nick couldn't help it. He just couldn't get his mouth to work.

A crash and a roar made the bearded giant look over Nick's head. Nick turned as the first giant broke into the clearing. The blue giant slobbered and scrambled toward them, bellowing as he came.

"Stay, Mogwoth," said the bearded giant calmly.

The blue giant slid to a stop, his bald head steaming. He stared at the new giant with wide eyes as a big glob of slobber dripped down the side of his mouth. "He's mine!" spat Mogwoth the Slobbering Giant.

The bearded giant's eyes narrowed. He pointed his axe at Mogwoth and said, "He's mine, what?"

Mogwoth bowed his head but kept his eyes hungrily on Nick. "He's mine, Your Majesty."

The bearded giant nodded. "That's better. Now wait your turn."

Mogwoth dipped his head again, sending a trail of spit into the snow. "Yes, King Thrym."

"Now," said King Thrym looking back at Nick with those intent green eyes. "Frost Giants don't normally eat rabbits like you but it appears Mogwoth wants to make an exception.

Give them to me and I'll order him not to harm you." He smiled. "Or at least give you a head start."

Talk of eating him unlocked Nick's jaw. "Give you what?" he finally said.

"What brought you here, of course," replied King Thrym.

"What do you mean?" asked Nick, desperate to avoid being munched but uncertain what the Giant King wanted.

"The talisman that brought you here," said King Thrym, smiling fiercely. "I want it."

Nick wasn't sure what "talisman" meant but he knew what had brought him here. He put a hand on his pocket and felt their rectangular outline. "You mean the cards? I have the cards," he said, hoping that was enough.

King Thrym's green eyes gleamed. "Then give them to me."

Nick stuck his half-frozen hand into his pocket and tried to pull out the deck. He had jammed the cards into his pocket sideways when the feather storm started and now they were stuck. He numbly fumbled around and tried to ignore the hungry stares of King Thrym and Mogwoth the Slobbering Giant but as you can imagine, being stared at like a turkey leg doesn't do much for your coordination. Finally, Nick yanked the cards free of his pocket but his hand was so frozen that he couldn't hold on and half of the deep blue deck scattered across the snow at King Thrym's feet.

King Thrym didn't seem to mind. As he reached out to pick up the cards, the Giant King smiled broadly and his green eyes glittered. His fingers touched the first card.

"Serpent's teeth!" he hissed and snatched his hand back as if he'd been bitten.

"What is it?!" cried Nick, afraid he'd done something that was about to make him a giant-sized happy meal.

"It burns," said King Thrym, his green eyes wide as he rubbed his great hand and stared at the scattered cards. "Like the coldest ice." He started to reach out again, then thought better of it. "Pick them up," he growled gruffly.

Nick bent and gathered the cards as quickly as he could, brushing snow off them as he went. He hastily sorted them, putting the backs with the MB shield up and the blank, light blue faces down.

"What are they?" King Thrym rumbled.

"Cards from a game my father gave me." Nick did not like the way King Thrym was looking at him so he hurried on. "But there's something wrong with them, look." Nick held the cards up as high as he could and fanned them out for the Giant King. "They're all blank."

King Thrym's gaze narrowed again and he seemed agitated as he continued to rub his hand. Nick thought this was bad. "But one of the cards wasn't," Nick continued. "It had me on it, and when I read it, I found myself here." Nick frantically shuffled through the deck until he found the red card back. He pulled it from the deck and held the Adventure Card up to King Thrym. "See?"

King Thrym bent down and peered closely. He reached out to take the Adventure Card but appeared to reconsider and carefully avoided touching it. "That's you, rabbit." His beard twitched. The Giant King stared at the cards, his eyes burning like bright green lasers. "What are the symbols under the picture?"

Nick looked at his Adventure Card again but only saw the words. "What symbols?"

"There. Those rows under the picture," said King Thrym, pointing, but not touching, the card.

"Oh, those are words. Letters."

"Ah, runes," mused King Thrym. "I can't read them," he muttered, still staring at the card. "This is the language of your home?"

"Yes."

"What does it say?"

"'Nick Snow had never seen it. That was about to change.'"

King Thrym grunted softly at that. "There are no other cards like this, rabbit?"

Nick shook his head.

"No other runes? No other pictures?" The Giant King pressed.

"No," said Nick. "They're all just solid blue."

"Just blue, just blue," muttered King Thrym, more to himself than to Nick. "I can't touch them but there's nothing to read, nothing to see. Nothing at all." He tapped his axe on the snow. "And that's how it needs to stay."

Nick grew afraid. When King Thrym had stopped Mogwoth, he'd thought maybe the Giant King was friendly. But as the Giant King muttered and as his green eyes flicked from Nick to Mogwoth and back to Nick again, Nick could see, as clearly as he saw the snow he was standing in, that King Thrym was not the least little bit friendly. Not at all.

King Thrym stood now, towering well above Nick. He flipped his axe in a circle and back onto his shoulder. "Well, Mogwoth," the Giant King said. "I thought young Snow here had something I needed. Turns out he doesn't." The Giant King shook his head as if in disappointment. "I seem to have interrupted your dinner. Sorry about that."

With that, the Giant King turned and walked away.

Nick had always been quick-witted (don't let his math grade fool you) and the moment he realized King Thrym was leaving, and what that departure meant, he sprinted away from Mogwoth. Mogwoth just sat there, seeming confused, as Nick ran toward the other end of the clearing. Nick barely looked as he high-stepped through the deep snow towards the woods. For a moment, he thought he'd make it.

Nick was still a good thirty yards from the trees when Mogwoth figured out his dinner was fleeing. Nick heard a roar and flicked a look over his shoulder to see Mogwoth charge him in an explosion of slobber and snow. Nick ran faster, getting closer to King Thrym (who was going in the same direction) and the trees. The Giant King turned back around at the commotion, looked at Nick, and smiled a green-eyed grin that would keep Nick up at night long after this Adventure was over. Then King Thrym took three giant steps, gripped his axe in both hands, and held it down low near his knees like a goalie's hockey stick. The Giant King was blocking Nick from the woods.

Mogwoth bellowed as he closed in on Nick. King Thrym chuckled as he blocked Nick's path with his axe. Nick veered to the left, hoping to avoid them both. The two giants matched Nick, preparing to catch him between them. All three screamed at once, one giant in a food frenzy, one Giant King in evil glee, and one kid in stark fear.

The sound of a horn blasted through the meadow, its high clear note piercing their screams. Nick recognized it as the same horn he'd heard when he first came to this frozen nightmare. The sound was deafening and all three instinctively stopped to look for the source of the blast.

A man stepped out of the woods, a horn in one hand, a drawn sword in the other. "Two warriors against one lad," he said, looking from Thrym to Nick to Mogwoth. "That hardly seems sporting. Even for giants."

Chapter 4

"You better leave Baldur," spat King Thrym. "Your momma's spell won't protect you here in my realm."

"Maybe so," replied the man Baldur, who didn't look the least bit concerned about facing the Giant King. "But when you crossed this meadow, you left the land of the giants and entered Midgard. And that," he said with a teeth-bearing grin that Nick found to be both good-natured and ferocious, "is a different story."

"This is not your problem," snarled King Thrym.

"Giants eating children most certainly is. No matter how strange looking they arc." Baldur gave Nick a quick wink, then turned back to King Thrym, his eyes fierce and his sword raised. "Now, go back to Jotunheim and your ice kingdom." He pointed his sword at Mogwoth. "I'm sure you have plenty of handsome subjects like this one who miss you."

Mogwoth snarled and took a giant step (literally) toward Baldur, but stopped when King Thrym raised his hand. "And good-natured too," said Baldur. "Charming. I can't imagine why you leave home."

King Thrym just stared at Baldur, his green eyes practically glowing with malice. "Ragnarok can't come soon enough," the Giant King said quietly.

"Bring it," was Baldur's reply.

The two stared at each other, their hands twitching on their weapons. And kept staring until it was quiet and tense and Nick was sure he was about to see some grade A head smacking. But to his surprise, King Thrym broke off first. "Come, Mogwoth," the Giant King said and walked towards the woods. Mogwoth gave Nick and Baldur one more slobbering snarl and tromped off behind King Thrym.

Nick watched the giants go. As they reached the edge of the clearing, warm relief washed over Nick as he realized he was alive and uneaten. Baldur turned his back on the giants and faced Nick, a kind but puzzled look on his face. "So . . ." he began.

A growl of rage cut him off. Nick ducked around Baldur in time to see Mogwoth rip a small tree from the ground, take two steps, and hurl it like a spear at Baldur's back. "Look out!" Nick yelled as the sapling flew in a perfect arc. Right for Baldur.

I am not exaggerating one bit when I tell you that Baldur never moved. He didn't even twitch. He just stared at Nick with that same kind but puzzled look, completely oblivious to the pine tree plummeting out of the sky to make a Baldur-kabob.

Nick didn't have time to warn Baldur again. He could only gasp as the twenty foot tree hurtled down and down, closer and closer to his new friend until, just as the tree was about to hit Baldur, at the very last moment, with not even an inch to spare. . .

. . . the tree jerked to the side and stuck point first in the snow, its long trunk quivering.

Nick looked at the tree, then back at Baldur in amazement. "Geezow!" said Nick. "It missed you! How did it miss you?!"

Baldur smiled. He had never even looked back.

Mogwoth the Slobberer howled (and slobbered). "Enough, Mogwoth," said King Thrym, coming back out of the woods and grabbing the blue giant by the arm. "That won't work. These trees are all oath-takers."

Mogwoth snarled and snapped a tree off at the trunk. "I feel the same way," King Thrym said. He cast one last look of green-eyed daggers at Baldur and Nick. "And eventually he will too." Then the Giant King dragged Mogwoth into the woods.

"Well, lad," said Baldur, without a glance at the twenty foot long tree-spear sticking out of the ground right next to him. "Who are you? And what do you have against giants?"

Nick didn't know what to say. He started to talk once, twice, and couldn't. He suddenly realized that he was standing in a mound of snow, that the sweat was freezing on his back, that he was wearing a thin, long-sleeved t-shirt that was torn in several places, and that he was terribly, terribly cold. His extreme physical discomfort, along with some lingering extreme fear, momentarily prevented him from realizing exactly what had just happened. In other words, it took Nick a moment to realize that he was now standing knee deep in a snow drift talking to a huge, sword-carrying, tree-proof man who had just kept a slobbering, pine-hurling giant from eating him.

So Nick just answered, "I don't know. Nothing. They seem to have something against me."

Baldur chuckled and smiled. "That they do, lad. The border between Jotunheim and Midgard is no place for a boy to travel alone." Baldur drove his great sword into the snow point first and rested an arm on the pommel. "I'm Baldur," he said, and extended a gloved hand to Nick.

Although still scared, Nick's parents had always insisted on good manners so he found it impossible to leave the man's hand hanging out there. "Nick Snow," he said and clasped Baldur's hand.

Baldur's eyes were curious again as they went from the back of Nick's hand to his shirt-sleeve. He held Nick's hand out to the side to get a better view of his t-shirt and jeans. "Nick Snow, you do not look like a boy from Midgard. What land are you from?"

"Florida," said Nick.

Baldur stared blankly at Nick. "I've never heard of this land. It is far from here?"

Nick had no idea where here was but, judging from the depth of the snow, knew it wasn't close to his home. "It's a ways," Nick said.

Baldur examined Nick with kind blue eyes and asked, "So where are you going, Nick Snow?"

Where am I going? he thought. How about somewhere warm where no one wants to eat me? "I don . . .I don't . . . I donnn'ttt-ttt-ttt kn-nn-nn-ow," said Nick with a voice that shivered and almost, but not quite, cried.

Baldur didn't appear to blame Nick anymore than you should. Instead, Baldur's brow furrowed, "You'll freeze lad, wet and dressed like that. Here," he said and twirled his grey fur cape off of his shoulders and around Nick's. "Don't worry, lad. You've had a fright and a freeze. You need fire and food. Then we'll figure out where you need to go."

Baldur turned to lead Nick out of the clearing but Nick didn't move. Nick's mom and dad had constantly drilled him on the danger of talking to strangers and he knew they would go nuts if he actually walked somewhere with one. So, for a moment, he didn't accept Baldur's offer. Of course, in all their endless lectures and constant warnings, Mom and Dad had never mentioned what to do if you were transported to a land of giants and were standing in a snow drift with no idea of where to go or what to do.

Though strangers were dangerous, Nick figured his parents would agree that kid-eating giants were too. Nick knew that he had barely escaped the Giant King and his minion and that the reason he had escaped was the man standing in front of him. And more than anything, Nick knew he needed help.

Which reminded him of another piece of parental advice. What did his mom and dad always say to do when he was lost or needed help? Talk to a policeman or a teacher. So he was allowed to talk to a stranger if the stranger was good and helped kids. But a woods was not a school, and it certainly wasn't a mall, and Nick didn't see any policemen or teachers. Someone who beats giants though . . .

"Are you good?" Nick asked finally.

"So they say," Baldur replied.

"Do you help kids?"

Baldur's smile broke into a wide, white grin. "I'm trying."

That was enough for Nick. "Okay. I'll go with you." Nick struggled to his feet against the weight and length of Baldur's cloak. "Let's go." He took one step forward, right on the bottom of the cloak, and tumbled headfirst into the snow.

Baldur laughed, an altogether pleasant sound that reminded Nick of church bells. "One moment, lad," he said. He picked up the back of the cloak and held it off the ground. "Keep it off the snow, Snow," he said with a smile.

"That's pretty bad," said Nick, smiling back.

"I know," Baldur grinned through his bushy red beard.

"It's actually kind of sad."

"Do you think so?"

"You're worse than my dad."

"That's low."

Nick giggled and thought for a moment. "I'm all out of 'ad's."

Baldur smiled back. "Then let's go."

Nick cracked up. And the two set off into the woods.

A short time later, Nick was bundled in Baldur's fur cloak, munching some dried meat as Baldur started a fire. Venison, Baldur had told him it was. Nick had never eaten deer jerky before and, two hours ago, he probably wouldn't have tried it, but right now it tasted better than a burger off Dad's grill. He ripped off another bite and chewed, his mouth tingling with tangy spices.

Nick burrowed deeper into Baldur's cloak, pulling the collar up around his neck to keep the wind off him, and watched Baldur feed sticks to a slowly growing fire. While he anxiously waited to feel its heat, Nick finally had a chance to study this man who cowed giants and deflected trees.

As he bent over the fire, Baldur's bushy red beard hung just above the flames. His thick red hair fell around his face but didn't cover blue eyes that flickered with humor and firelight. Even crouched over the fire, Nick could see Baldur was tall (not giant tall but human tall) and his steel helmet, complete with white horns sticking out the side, made him seem even taller. Now that he'd given Nick his cloak, he wore leather boots, brown leather pants, and a loosely-tied leather vest that left his massive arms bare to the cold (which Baldur didn't seem to mind in the least). A sword was belted at his hip and a silver horn hung from his shoulder. Around his left arm, just above his bicep, he wore a ring of braided metal that was so silver it was almost white. The center of the ring was shaped like two wolves' heads growling at each other and their open mouths held a sparkling ruby the size of a quarter. Nick had never seen anything like it. Or like Baldur.

"Well, Nick Snow," said Baldur with a sigh. Nick looked away from the armring as the big man plopped down next to him. Baldur pulled off his horned helmet and shook out long red hair that reached past his shoulders. He scratched his thick beard and looked from the roaring fire back to Nick. "If you don't mind me saying, for someone named Snow, you don't seem very prepared for it. Your clothes would barely keep you warm in summer."

Nick shivered and nodded, pulling the fur cloak around him a little tighter.

Baldur nodded back, his eyes kind and his voice quiet. "So why are you here, lad?"

Nick stared, uncertain what to say. Well Baldur, he thought, my dad bought me a new card game and when I opened it there was an Adventure Card with my picture on it and a featherstorm whirled me away to your snow-covered, giant-filled forest. Nick thought that sounded too ridiculous to say, even to someone who would believe the giant part. Besides, technically, that answered how he got here, not why. So Nick said what he usually did when a bunch of answers were swirling around in his head.

"I don't know."

"Well, where are you going then?" asked Baldur.

Since he didn't know where here was, Nick couldn't say where in the here he was going. So again he said, "I don't know."

"That makes it harder to get there," said Baldur. "What are you looking for?"

Nick felt his eyes well-up. It was the first time they'd felt warm since he'd been here. "My way home," he said, and though he hated it, and though he tried not to, he quietly began to cry.

A look of sympathy crossed Baldur's face and he put one massive hand lightly on Nick's shoulder. "Your home is far from here, lad?" he asked gently. Nick nodded.

"And it is warm there?"

Nick nodded again.

"And you came here suddenly?"

Nick nodded a third time.

"Then maybe your way back will be sudden as well."

Nick felt a warm rush of hope at the thought. A moment later, the cold realization of his predicament snuffed it out. "How do I find it? My way home?" he said quietly and wiped an eye before a tear could freeze to his cheek.

"I don't know," it was Baldur's turn to say. "How did you get here? Maybe you can return the same way."

Here goes, thought Nick. I'll have to tell him about the cards, no matter how ridiculous it sounds. The cards! Momentarily panicked that he'd lost them, Nick slapped at his baggy pants until he felt their rectangular outline. Relieved, he pulled the deck out of his pocket and fanned through the ice blue Norse deck until he saw the fire red card back.

"I'm not sure how, but I'm pretty sure the Adventure Card did it," Nick said, pulling the red card out of the deck.

"The Adventure Card?" Baldur frowned.

"It was in a game my dad gave me. I opened the deck and one of the cards was different from the others. It had my picture on it and when I read it, I ended up here. See?"

Nick flipped the red card over and there he was on the other side. Same grey shirt. Same baggy jeans.

"That's you, lad." Baldur peered closely at the card. "The runes under your picture. What do they say?"

Nick realized Baldur couldn't read the cards either. "'*Nick Snow had never seen it,*'" he said. "'*That was about to change. The Adventure Card is the Key. Brace yourself.*'" I would have braced myself if I'd had any idea what was going on, he thought. But I didn't have time before the goosefeather-storm started.

Baldur considered what Nick had said for a moment. "'The Adventure Card is the Key.' That's the Adventure Card?"

"It must be. That's what it says on the back." Nick flipped the card around to show Baldur.

"So maybe that card is your key to getting home."

"Do you think? It's just part of a game."

"Do games usually transport men in your land, lad?"

Nick shook his head.

"Then it must be something more."

"Maybe," said Nick. "But all I did before was read it and it sent me here. This is the second time I've looked at it since I've been here, and I'm still here, if you know what I mean. See?" Nick flipped it around a couple more times. "Nothing. It's just a card."

"Well, you're here so that can't be completely true," said Baldur. He thought for a moment. "Is the rest of it true?"

"About the snow?" said Nick. "Yeah. Never saw it 'till today."

Baldur raised his eyebrows. "There's no winter in this Florida?"

"Sure. It gets all the way down to sixty degrees." Baldur raised his eyebrows a little more. Nick struggled to explain temperature readings to a man in a land without a weather channel or thermometers. Finally, he said, "It only rains, the water never freezes, and these clothes are too warm there."

Baldur's eyebrows rose even more. "How do you know when it's harvest time? Or when a herd of deer have passed?" Baldur shook his head. "I don't think I'd know I was alive if I couldn't see my breath in the morning."

"That's what almost got me killed," said Nick. "My breath. I hid behind a tree but the slobbering giant saw my breath."

"Breathe into your shirt next time," said Baldur with less sympathy than Nick expected. Baldur's brow furrowed. "How long ago did you come here? Did Mogwoth find you right away?"

Nick nodded. "It was just a little bit ago. The slobbering giant started chasing me as soon as I plopped into the snow." Nick shivered again at the memory of his fear-filled run through the woods.

Baldur abruptly looked away from the card to Nick. "Why did you stop?" he asked suddenly.

"Stop?" asked Nick. He didn't know what Baldur was talking about.

"When Mogwoth chased you into the clearing where King Thrym was," said Baldur. "Why did you stop?"

Nick looked down at the fire. "I wouldn't have gotten away," he said quietly.

"You don't know that," said Baldur. "There were little paths between trees, under bushes. Trails a giant wouldn't take. You could have kept running."

"The giants just would have caught me."

"You have to try."

"You sound like my dad."

"Your father sounds like a wise man," Baldur said with a smile.

Nick shrugged.

Nick could feel Baldur studying him. "It's okay to be scared you know," Baldur said. "You just can't let it freeze you. You have to use the fear to make you move faster."

"What, so I'll be digested quicker?"

Baldur chuckled at that and patted Nick again on the shoulder. "Sometimes it's more important to try than to win."

Baldur paused. "I don't know how to send you home, lad," he said finally. "Right now the card's not sending you back but I'd keep it close anyway. It's the only clue we have."

Baldur stopped and turned to stare at the now roaring fire. He seemed to be thinking and Nick decided that was a good idea for at least one of them. Nick put the Adventure Card back in the deck and put the deck back in his pocket. Then he accepted another piece of jerky from Baldur, started munching again, and waited. James Snow was very big on not interrupting grown-ups and this seemed like the perfect time to practice it.

"You'll need to cross the bridge," said Baldur finally.

"The bridge?" asked Nick.

"Bifrost. The bridge to Asgard. You'll need to cross it," said Baldur matter-of-factly.

"Why do I need to cross the Bifrost bridge?"

"You'll have to cross to talk to my father. He's the only one I can think of who might know how to help you."

"Your father?" asked Nick.

"Odin," Baldur said with a smile.

Nick stared blankly at Baldur, not recognizing the name. Baldur raised an eyebrow. "The All-Father? Big man, one-eye, couple of crows always hanging around?" Nick shook his head.

Baldur abruptly laughed, a deep rumble that seemed to pour mirth from his entire body. "Your home must be very far away." His laughter trickled to a chuckle. "Odin is the lord of the gods. Maybe he can help you." Baldur chuckled again. "Though I wouldn't tell him that he's not known in your land."

"I'll tell him I go to Odin Elementary on All-Father Avenue if it will get me home. Just tell me how to. . . . What the. . . ?"

As he'd spoken, Nick's pocket started to vibrate. He stuck his hand in. It was the deck. As he pulled it out, it stopped. Curious, he flipped the deck around. The card back hadn't changed. The light blue side had.

There was a picture on it.

On what had been a blank blue card, there was now a picture of a grey-bearded man wearing an eye-patch and carrying a crow on each shoulder. "Odin" was written in the top corner. Nick quickly scanned the words under the picture:

> *The "All-Father" rules Asgard on the other side of the rainbow bridge. Add 10 to the scores of Hunin and Munin, his crows, Freki and Geri, his wolves, and Sleipnir, his horse, when he is on the field at the same time as one of them.*

"What is it?" asked Baldur, hovering over Nick's shoulder.

"A game card," said Nick, still staring. "Of Odin. Just like with the Egyptian deck." Nick quickly checked the rest of the deck. The other cards were still blank. "But it's the only one."

"I can't read those runes. What does it say?"

"Exactly what you said. That Odin the All-Father rules Asgard on the other side of the rainbow bridge."

Baldur smiled. "Well that settles it then. I'll take you to the bridge. And to Odin."

"Thanks," Nick said with relief. But a last wave of caution welled-up before he agreed. "Why would you do that?"

"Your skin is dark, your clothes are light, and your home is warm and far. A strange tale surrounds you, Nick Snow, like none I've heard since the thaw. I would hear the end of your tale and you won't be able to tell it if you don't make it to Odin." Baldur's blue eyes smiled but they were kind. "Besides, I'm not about to let a lad like you wander around by himself."

"Why wouldn't I make it to Odin?" asked Nick.

"Because if I don't guide you, you may wander into Jotunheim or walk too close to Fenris Wolf."

"Jotunheim?" asked Nick.

"The land of the giants. We're very close to it. Thrym is one of its kings."

Blink. "A wolf?"

"Not just a wolf. Fenris Wolf. He guards the Bifrost."

"The Bifrost. That's the bridge we're crossing?"

"Yes."

"And there's a wolf guarding it?"

"Exactly. And you don't want to get too close him. He bit off a god's hand once."

Blink. Blink. "You've passed the wolf?"

"Many times."

"I think you should guide me."

"I agree," said Baldur with a smile.

Now you shouldn't think that Nick felt at all good about being stranded in this cold land of Midgard. But just then, he felt a little bit better.

Chapter 5

Once he decided to accept Baldur's help, Nick couldn't wait to get going. As his grandmother said, "it was time to blow this popsicle stand," and in all his short life, he couldn't think of a more frozen, popsically place he'd like to leave.

"Let's go then," Nick said and struggled to his feet against the weight and length of Baldur's cloak. He took one step forward and stumbled again on the bottom of the cloak. He wrestled the heavy fur up to his knees and staggered another step.

"Wait, wait lad," Baldur chuckled. "The Bifrost doesn't move and Heimdall will be waiting for us whenever we get there. Let me fix that cloak first."

Baldur took the gray fur cloak which, from his nature TV viewing, Nick guessed to be wolf or fox. He could even make out a few tails sewn into the fabric although, thankfully, no animal eyes stared back at him. As Baldur set to work, he reminded Nick of a clown he'd once seen make balloon animals at a birthday party; the clown had started with a thin blue balloon, then he'd blown, bent, twisted, squeaked, honked and—Ta-Da!—the clown had held up a little blue dog. Now Baldur started with a long grey cloak, a knife, and a handful of leather strips, and then he cut, tied, bound, wrapped and—Ta-Da!—Nick was standing in a fur hat, a tightly wrapped cloak, fur mittens, and fur leggings.

"I can't do anything for your shoes," Baldur said as he gave a final tug on a strap around Nick's leg. He sheathed his knife and shook his head. "Your feet will be cold and wet by the time we reach the bridge."

Nick hardly cared. He just knew that for the first time since he'd arrived, he was warm. And even more important— nothing was cooler than being dressed in wolf pelts. If only Chris could see this. "It's fine," he said, setting aside coolness to remember his manners. "Thank you."

"Moving water doesn't freeze," Baldur said. "Let's go." And with that, the two set off for the bridge Baldur named the Bifrost.

★ ★ ★

The soft snow rose knee high on Nick, and I doubt I need to tell you how hard that is to walk through, especially for an eleven-year-old bundled in wolf skins. Baldur must have known it too because he led Nick down a path where the snow had been trampled hard by many boots.

Even with the firmer path, Nick had to hustle along at a half-trot to keep up with his new guide. Baldur was well over six feet tall, seven if you counted the horns on his helmet. His long strides ate up an awful lot of ground, making his long, red hair stream behind him like flames and his white breath roll back like smoke.

Since he had given Nick his cloak, Baldur only wore a leather vest and his red-rubied armring. No heavy shirt, no armor. Nick thought this was strange since people in the snow usually got cold and people who carried swords usually got swung at. Neither the low temperature nor his lack of defenses seemed to bother Baldur though as they walked down the path, with Nick scampering to keep up and Baldur looking down every few steps to smile encouragement.

Nick was concentrating so hard on keeping up that he barely noticed the two enormous oak trees that straddled the path. "You'll need to stay back a few steps, lad," Baldur said as soon as they passed the trees.

Nick cast a nervous glance over his shoulder, back toward where the giants had been. "Why?" he said.

Baldur followed Nick's backwards glance and laughed. "We're in a different part of Midgard now, lad. We're getting closer to the bridge. And the gods."

"So?"

"You just stay a few steps away from me. Make it to the side if you don't want to be behind me." And with that Baldur stepped off the path and began wading through the snow. That slowed Baldur just enough for Nick to be able to keep up without trotting and talk without panting. Which led him to ask, "So you think Odin will know how to help me?"

Baldur pushed smoothly through the deep snow as he answered, "Odin knows most of what happens in Midgard. His crows Hugin and Munin see all of Midgard from their perch on his shoulders. His wolves, Freki and Geri, hear all that happens in Midgard as they curl at his feet." Baldur threw a smile over to Nick. "You stand out, Nick Snow. My guess is that they've noticed what's happened to you. And that Odin may know what to do about it."

Nick was momentarily self-conscious and dropped his gaze to the snow. "Lad," Baldur said. Nick looked back up and Baldur met his eyes. "The unnoticed ground is trod upon while all walk around the upright pine."

Nick tried to wrap his brain around that one then shook his head. "What?" he asked.

Baldur smiled. "Standing out is good."

Nick started to reply when he heard a whoosh. A second later, snow exploded into the air in front of Baldur's feet and words Nick wasn't supposed to know exploded out of his mouth. Baldur, with a look of tired amusement, held up a hand to Nick. "Hold still," he said. "There's usually a few of them."

Nick had no idea what "them" were but he knew that "they" were moving awfully fast. Nick stared at Baldur, frozen. All of a sudden there was a Whoosh! Whoosh! And two more clouds of snow erupted at Baldur's feet.

Nick realized he was hearing whatever "they" were buzz through the air, like the way you hear a good pitch zip through the air before it hits the catcher's glove. But this was faster, much faster, than anything he'd ever heard (or seen) before, faster even than when Nick's dad had taken him to a Florida Marlins game and they'd watched the pitcher warm up in the bullpen.

Now that he recognized that the whoosh was something cutting through the air, Nick pivoted around, searching for the source of attack. He looked skyward in time to see two stones streaking down from the clouds. Right for Baldur.

"Baldur!" he cried. "Duck!"

Baldur didn't move as the stones bee-lined straight at his head. Nick started to yell again, knowing it was too late. But then, right before the stones hit Baldur, they turned away from him and plunged down onto the ground in front of him, sending up a shower of snow. "What the . . ." Nick said.

Before he had time to think, a large stick tumbled out of the sky, whirling end over end at Baldur. To stunned to yell, Nick just stood there as the stick flew towards Baldur . . . and snapped to the earth in front of him like it had hit a force field.

Baldur stood still, hand raised. Nick did the same, searching the sky. Nothing else came.

"That should do it," Baldur said finally. He pointed a finger at Nick. "And that's why you need to stay over there."

"What the heck was that?" said Nick.

"Sticks and stones," said Baldur.

To anyone else, Nick would have said, "Duh." To his new enormous Norse friend, he said, "I know what they were. How did they miss? They were headed right for you." The near misses reminded Nick of something else. "It was just like in the clearing when Mogwoth threw that tree at you. It was headed right for your back and then at the last second it missed, like it turned to the side."

Baldur stared at Nick for a second. Then he sighed and started walking next to the path again. "Let's walk while we talk. We've got a ways to go and I want to reach the bridge by nightfall. Just stay over there."

As the two set off again, Nick watched Baldur out of the corner of his eye, amazed but not wanting to stare. Baldur began. "Frigga is my mother. One night, she dreamt that I had died. The dream was so powerful and so real that when she woke up, she couldn't shake the dream and became convinced that I was going to be killed. So she did what any concerned mother would do."

"Made you stay in the house?" Nick guessed.

"No. She made everything in the world promise not to harm me."

And Nick thought he'd been embarrassed when his mom called his friend's parents before a sleepover. Sheesh! Imagine having your mom going to all the things in the world and asking them not to hurt her precious little boy.

"Don't start!" said Baldur, his hand still up. "I get it enough from my brothers." Baldur paused as if waiting for Nick to ask questions. Fortunately for us, Nick asked them.

"Who is Frigga?" asked Nick.

"My mother," replied Baldur.

"No, I heard that. I mean, how could she do that?" asked Nick.

"She's a god."

"Okay."

"And she's married to Odin."

"Ah." Nick only half heard Baldur's explanation. His pocket was vibrating again. He pulled out the deck just as it stopped. He immediately looked at the card faces.

A second card had appeared. This one said "Frigga" and had a picture of a woman with long blond braids. Beneath it was written:

> *The wife of Odin was also the protector of Baldur. While she is on the field, Baldur cannot be attacked.*

"What is it?" asked Baldur.

"Another card. Frigga this time."

"What does this one say?"

Nick told him.

"Great," Baldur snorted. "Even kids' games from the land of the sun know about it."

"Is it that bad?" asked Nick.

"It's embarrassing," Baldur replied.

They trudged in the snow for a bit as Nick digested this information. "She really went to everything in the world?"

"So she says."

"But to find them all, to talk to each thing . . ." Nick trailed off in disbelief.

"She's very persistent," Baldur said, and Nick heard the resigned tone of a son who knew it very well.

Nick thought some more about what he'd seen, about the rocks and sticks seemingly flying at them from nowhere. "So where'd they come from, the rocks?"

"The gods throw them."

Nick looked over at Baldur. "What do you mean the gods throw them?"

Baldur shrugged. "They all know what my mother did. A while back, someone tested it and threw a rock at me." He smiled through his red beard. "Ever since, there's been nothing more fun than bouncing rocks off Baldur."

You have to remember everything that had just happened to Nick. When you do, you'll realize why it wasn't hard for Nick to believe Baldur's incredible explanation (and don't forget, he'd seen a small tree turn away too). "Doesn't that bug you?" Nick said finally.

"A little," said Baldur, nodding. "But it's all in fun and you do sort of get used to it." He checked Nick again. "I just have to make sure my traveling companions stay at a safe distance. Things have a tendency to bounce off. Or splatter."

"Splatter?" Nick asked.

"Sometimes its mud. Or livestock."

"Eehck," said Nick.

"So just stay over there. There will be more the closer we get to Asgard."

As if on cue, an ax handle tumbled end over end out of the sky, straight toward Baldur. It bounced to the side and landed between him and Nick.

"I think I'll stay over here," said Nick with a smile.

Nick and Baldur followed the path through the woods for most of the day. Or, we should say that Nick walked on the path and Baldur walked next to the path with stones pinging off him at regular intervals. By late afternoon, Nick was getting pretty tired. Then the woods ended and the two stepped free of the trees.

Snow-covered mountains rose directly ahead of them. A towering wall of jagged white peaks stretched to his left and right as far as Nick could see. The sun was sinking at the left edge of the mountains, so Nick knew the incredible range must be to the north. Nick, from the flat marshes of Florida, had never seen anything like it.

But the mountains weren't what made him gasp. The rainbow did.

One end of a great rainbow rested directly in front of them. Enormous bands of color shot out of the earth and arced high into the air and straight over the mountains. Red, orange, yellow, green, blue, indigo, violet. Just like in science class when they did the experiment with the prism. But this wasn't a little fleck of light cast on a black school table. This rainbow was deep and vibrant and shimmered in the light of setting sun. And unlike any rainbow he'd ever seen, this one seemed solid, without the slightest transparency, giving no hint of what lay on the other side.

"The Bifrost bridge," said Baldur. "I'm glad we made it before sunset. I didn't want to sleep in the woods."

Nick looked around puzzled. "Where's the bridge? Behind the rainbow?"

"Florida must be very, very far away." Baldur smiled. "The Bifrost isn't behind the rainbow, lad. It is the rainbow. That is our bridge to Asgard."

Now you shouldn't be surprised that Nick finally started to doubt what Baldur was telling him. He was perfectly willing to believe in man-eating giants, all-seeing crows, peace-promising rocks. But a rainbow bridge? He was pretty sure that Baldur was just making fun of him.

"That's our bridge," Nick said in a half-questioning, half-sarcastic tone.

"To Asgard," replied Baldur cheerily.

"How are we supposed to cross a rainbow bridge?" asked Nick, still thinking that Baldur was playing a joke on him. "With a bowl of Lucky Charms?"

"We don't need charms or magic," Baldur replied. "We'll just talk to the bridge-keeper."

"What, is there some little guy in a green suit hiding in a pot somewhere?"

Baldur looked puzzled. "No. I mean Heimdall. Right over there."

Nick followed Baldur's gaze to the left of the rainbow where a huge man was striding towards them. A great shield was strapped to his back, a great horn hung at his side, and as he approached, it looked to Nick like he was about to draw the great sword at his belt. When he got closer though, a great smile broke across his face. He immediately ducked to the ground, grabbed two enormous handfuls of snow, and then hurled a snowball as big as a bowling ball at Baldur's head. It missed him.

"Guess he recognized you," said Nick.

"Fortunately Heimdall's eyes are sharper than his aim," replied Baldur.

"That's not fair," said Nick, grinning. "You cheat."

Baldur's eyes danced as he smiled in return. "Only a little."

"Giants, Baldur," boomed Heimdall as he finally stopped before them. "Have you seen any giants?"

"A couple," said Baldur.

"Are they attacking?" Heimdall asked hopefully.

"Not any more."

"Bragh. Too bad." Heimdall's face fell with such disappointment that Nick almost laughed. "I haven't seen any. Not a one. Well, except for Loki when he came through a little bit ago but he hardly counts." Then his face brightened. "Do you think they'll try later?"

"Attacking?"

"Yes."

"Almost certainly."

"Well that's something then," Heimdall said with a smile. Heimdall went from smiling at Baldur to staring at Nick. "What's this?" he asked.

"This is my friend, Nick Snow," said Baldur with a wave of his hand. Baldur turned to Nick. "Heimdall is the Watchman of the Gods. He guards the bridge to Asgard against the giants."

"The big uglies haven't attacked yet but when they do, I'll finally get to sound this baby," Heimdall said, patting the horn that hung at his side. The large, curved bull's horn was as long as Nick's arm and twice as big around. It was hollowed out at the wide end with a silver mouthpiece at the small, pointed end, and bands of red gold were spaced evenly between them. "Sound it?" Nick asked.

Heimdall looked at Nick in surprise. "Sound it. Blow it."

"Is it a horn?" Nick asked.

"It isn't *a* horn," snorted Heimdall. "It's the Giallar Horn." Heimdall seemed to really see Nick for the first time. "Where are you from?"

"Florida."

Heimdall stared at him. "Are there giants in Florida?"

"No," said Nick. "How do you use it?"

"I told you. You blow it. Have you no horns in Florida?"

"Not like that," said Nick, shaking his head.

Heimdall laughed. "There wouldn't be. There are none like the Giallar Horn in all of Midgard. Or Asgard or Jotunheim. When the giants finally invade, I'll blow this horn so loud it'll knock the leaves off every tree in Asgard. Then the gods and heroes will come for Ragnarok and we will have such a battle. . . ." He broke off with a sigh and patted the horn with the faraway expression of a kid contemplating a birthday party that was still months away.

"Against the giants?" asked Nick.

"Of course the giants." Heimdall looked questioningly at Nick. "There are really no giants in Florida?"

"No. They're all in New York."

"Then you haven't fought the giants yet either?" Heimdall asked. Nick shook his head. Heimdall continued, smiling with that same faraway expression, "Nor us. But we will. And our battle against the giants at Ragnarok will be the greatest battle Midgard has ever seen."

Heimdall stared dreamily at the sky for a moment. Then he snapped his eyes around to Nick, fully focused. "Of course it will also mean the end of the world. But no reason to talk about that now. You didn't come here to talk about horns and giant wars."

Heimdall looked from Nick to Baldur to Nick to Baldur to Nick. "Why did you come here?"

"To see Odin," said Baldur. Baldur seemed amused by the Watchman's running thoughts and conversation. "To see if he can help our lad Snow here find his way home."

"Ah, to this giant-less Florida place," said Heimdall. "An excellent idea." Heimdall waved his hand. "You know the way. Just stay extra clear of Fenris today. He's been all riled up since Loki came through earlier. Good day to you, Nick Snow. I hope ol' One Eye can help you."

"Thanks," said Nick, but by the time he said it, Heimdall was already walking away, humming cheerily and tapping his horn.

"Heimdall's alone a lot," said Baldur, following Nick's gaze. "He gets chatty when he has visitors." He smiled. "Let's go. The bridge is just ahead."

The two started toward rainbow. Nick remembered what Heimdall had said. "Who's Fenris again?" he asked.

"The wolf who guards the bridge."

Nick stopped. His heart beat right out of his chest. "Baldur. How do you cross the bridge?"

Baldur stared at Nick calmly. "Simple. You walk past him."

Chapter 6

Everyone has a bad dog experience but Nick's was worse than most. He'd gone to his aunt and uncle's house to play with his cousin, Jeff. Uncle Steve and Jeff had just let Nick in the front door when their Siberian Husky, Buck, had come around the corner from the kitchen. Although Nick had been a little nervous around Buck at first (the different colored eyes were spooky), he'd gotten used to him over the two years they'd had him and he held out his hand, fist clenched, just like he'd been taught. No one was ever sure why it happened but Buck took one sniff, ripped past Uncle Steve and went straight for Nick's leg. Buck knocked Nick down, bit his knee right through his pants, and dragged Nick across the room, shaking him furiously as they went. It had taken Jeff and Uncle Steve almost a minute to pull the suddenly insane, growling dog off him. Which may not sound like a very long time until you imagine a growling, shaking, fang-biting, knee-ripping minute.

So you shouldn't be surprised when I tell you that Nick was not at all happy to hear about the wolf. In fact, as he walked toward the rainbow with Baldur, Nick thought his heart might burst. His legs felt weak and his head light at the thought of walking past a wolf. Not a dog, mind you, but an honest to goodness wolf. Still, when Baldur stopped him,

Nick had almost convinced himself that he was being silly, that it wouldn't be too bad, that the wolf was far worse in his head than in real life.

Until he saw the wolf.

Fenris Wolf lay directly in front of the rainbow bridge. He was bigger than a horse and his black fur blocked the vivid colors of the rainbow like a violent storm cloud. His yellow eyes glowed and surveyed Nick as if he were a particularly tempting and tasty rabbit. The wolf didn't move, but Nick felt like he was just waiting until Nick came into range. Nick could not see how they would ever get past it.

Nick and Fenris Wolf stared at each other for a moment. Nick found himself inching closer to Baldur. Fenris Wolf didn't move. "Why isn't he charging us?" asked Nick.

"He is bound."

"By what?"

"The Gleipnir chain."

Nick didn't see any chain. Then he looked closer and saw a thin, faint, light, wholly inadequate chain. "What is it made of, steel?"

Baldur snorted. "Steel won't hold Fenris Wolf."

"Then what's the chain made of?"

"The noise of a footfall of a cat, the beards of women, the roots of stone, the breath of fishes, the nerves of bears, and the spit of birds."

Nick stared at Baldur. "You're kidding."

"No," Baldur said.

"You left out a pile of baloney."

Baldur shrugged off Nick's disbelief. "The Gleipnir Chain's thin links are unbreakable. It's the only chain in all of Asgard or Midgard that could hold Fenris Wolf."

Nick didn't think he could take another step forward. Fenris Wolf made Buck look like a fluffy puppy. So he stalled. "How did they get the chain on him?" he asked.

Baldur spoke but never took his eyes off the wolf. "First the gods offered it to him as a gift. It's beautiful but Fenris wasn't fooled and refused it. The gods kept after him though (I mentioned how persistent my mother can be) and Fenris finally agreed to try on the chain on one condition—he would let the gods put the chain around his neck if one of the gods put his hand in Fenris Wolf's mouth. Then, when the gods took the chain back off, Fenris would release the god's hand."

Nick stared at the wolf. He could not imagine anything that would make him put his hand in the wolf's mouth.

Baldur nodded as if sensing Nick's thoughts. "None of the gods were to keen on the idea either. But then Tyr, the god of war, stepped up and volunteered to guarantee the wolf's release. With his hand."

Baldur shook his head. "Few acts match the courage of that one. Tyr put his hand in Fenris Wolf's mouth and the gods looped the chain around the wolf's neck. Once it was done, the gods decided it was worth the cost to keep Fenris Wolf bound." He looked at Nick, his lips pressed tightly behind his red beard for a moment as if thinking.

"What happened?" asked Nick.

"Tyr is now the one-handed god of war," Baldur said. Unable to help himself, Nick shuddered. Right then, Fenris Wolf yawned hugely, exposing massive white teeth.

"The gods took the chain, tied Fenris Wolf to the bridge here, and forced him to guard it for them," Baldur continued, staring at the wolf. "He does it. But he doesn't like it and I have a feeling he's just waiting for the day when Heimdall will finally blow his horn."

Nick looked the question at Baldur. "Remember what Heimdall said about Ragnarok?" Baldur asked. "The battle at the end of time when the giants will attack the gods?"

Nick nodded.

"When Ragnarok comes, Fenris Wolf will be freed." Baldur stared at the wolf with an intensity Nick hadn't seen before. "He will fight with the giants."

Fenris Wolf stared back with a calm yellow gaze. Nick got the impression the wolf understood every word. And couldn't wait.

"But enough stories," said Baldur, looking back at Nick. "It's time to cross."

Nick couldn't take his eyes off the horse-sized wolf blocking the bridge. "How?" he said.

Baldur put a hand on Nick's shoulder. "You must walk past the wolf, lad."

Without realizing, Nick started shaking his head and pulling back. "No way," he said.

Baldur didn't squeeze but the weight of his hand kept Nick next to him. "He can't reach you."

"Did that ax handle hit you in the head? He'll kill me!"

"He won't."

"I can hear the TV now."

"We must cross the bridge, lad."

"Nick Snow, eleven years old, was eaten by a wolf today."

"The bridge is the only way to Odin."

"He walked right up to it and was ripped to shreds."

"It's the only way to get you home."

"Witnesses have no idea why he did something so stupid."

"You must pass."

Nick looked at Baldur, pleading. "I can't." Nick had never meant something so much in his whole short life.

Baldur squatted down so his eyes were level with Nick's. His voice was kind, but completely unrelenting. "You can. Only your fear is stopping you."

"That's easy for you to say. There's no reason for you to be afraid. Nothing can hurt you."

A strange look crossed Baldur's face. "There are other things to fear besides being hurt." Baldur shook his head and his blue eyes refocused on Nick. "It doesn't matter what it is you fear. Whatever it is, you must face the fear or it will chase you forever."

Nick started. His dad had said the same thing a couple of hours (and a couple of worlds) ago. And at that moment, Nick missed his dad very much.

"We must cross," said Baldur firmly. He put an arm around Nick's shoulder and turned him back toward the bridge.

"Walk straight toward the red band," he said, pointing at the band of color that was the farthest to the left. "The wolf can't reach you so long as you walk straight at the red."

"You'll walk next to me?" Nick asked.

Baldur shook his head. "I'll walk behind you. There is only room for one at a time to cross."

"Then why don't you go first?"

"Because it's safe on the other side, in Asgard. It's not safe here."

Nick searched Baldur's face for the slightest hint that he could get out of this. He saw none.

Instead, Baldur continued. Calmly. Remorselessly. "I'm telling you that you will pass. The wolf cannot hurt you if you stay in the red. The only thing hurting you is the fear in your heart, a fear of something you imagine will happen, a fear of something I'm telling you will not happen. Would you be trapped in Midgard forever by your imagination? Would you be barred from your home by the breath of a wolf? By his bark? Will you hesitate to do great things for fear of shadows?"

Nick felt like Baldur was staring right through him. His blue eyes held Nick. "Have you courage, Nick Snow?" he asked.

No, thought Nick. But he didn't want to stay here, in this icy land of giants. And he didn't want to keep standing in front of this wolf. And, surprisingly, he discovered he didn't want to disappoint Baldur.

Nick turned and faced the wolf. *The* Wolf—Fenris Wolf, Guardian of the Bridge to Asgard and Eater of Tyr's Right Hand. Nick took a deep breath. Then he took a step forward. It was, up to now, the bravest thing he'd ever done.

"Good lad," said Baldur softly. "Now forward, slowly. Walk straight toward the red."

Nick's heart pounded in his ears. His legs shook with each step. His hands clenched with each ragged breath. But he moved forward. He kept walking, straight toward the red, hoping that Baldur was behind him but too scared to look.

Fenris Wolf's ears pricked forward as Nick approached (Nick told me later he was sure the wolf could hear his heart). When Nick was ten feet away, Fenris Wolf stood. The wolf towered over Nick, a monster of black fur and yellow eyes. The wolf's tongue lolled out from between curved white teeth and licked the side of his mouth. The wolf walked across the front of the rainbow, past the violet and indigo, past the blue and green, its razor claws clicking on the stones. It came to the orange band of the rainbow, its black bulk blocking all the other colors from Nick's view. All except the red. Nick stopped. So did Fenris Wolf.

"Stand back Fenris, you puny cur!" Nick jumped at Baldur's shout. "This is Nick Snow of Florida, a confounder of giants and guest of Odin! We'll pass and we'll have none of your posing or I'll have Thor shorten your chain by a link or two."

Fenris growled at that, a low rumble more like a lion than a wolf. Nick wasn't sure, but it seemed to him that Fenris took a half step back. Nick started again.

As he put one foot in front of the other, Nick felt Baldur's hand clasp his shoulder. That firm pressure steadied him as came up to Fenris Wolf.

The wolf leaned forward, lowering its head to Nick's level. It dug its claws into the ground, crouched, and strained against the chain. The thin links gouged a crease into the wolf's fur as it pulled tight against its neck. The wolf's nose stopped just short of the red band.

Nick kept his eyes fixed on the red band as he walked. He heard the rasp of the wolf's harsh panting. He felt the heat of the wolf's ragged breath on the side of his face. He smelled the foulness of the wolf's last meal, though what it had been he dared not imagine.

Most importantly, he kept walking.

When Nick had almost reached the bridge, Fenris Wolf let out a howl. Without thinking, Nick yelled and dove straight for the red band of the rainbow. And before you say you could have done better, you'd need to hear that howl, a howl of anger at being bound for hundreds of years, a howl of hunger at being denied a tasty young Floridian, and a howl of anticipation of the day of his release. Then you'd need to hear that howl right next to your ear from a horse-sized wolf that slobbered on the side of your face when he did it. Personally, I don't think most of you would have done half so well as Nick (and I think quite a few of you would need to change your pants afterwards).

When Nick dove at the red band of the rainbow, he just wanted to get away from Fenris Wolf. He had no idea how the bridge worked. The Bifrost looked so solid that he'd just sort of figured that they would walk up it and cross over to Asgard. It didn't happen that way.

The second Nick hit the red band, the howling stopped. He sank into a wall of red and was surrounded by red light. He couldn't feel Baldur's hand anymore. Either he started to move or his head started to spin because he couldn't tell up from down. The red whirled around him until the venison jerky rose in his throat. Then, before he could spit out the jerky, the rainbow spat him onto the ground.

He landed face first. Soft grass caught him. Nick lifted his head to find himself in a sunlit golden field. It felt warm. Not Florida warm, but finally, at long last, warm. He heard a chuckle.

Nick turned to find that the rainbow was now behind him. Baldur stood, hands on hips chuckling. "Not exactly what I had in mind, lad. But bravely done. I've seen grown men fare worse."

Baldur bent over and held out a hand to Nick. Nick took it. Baldur pulled Nick up and brushed the stems of grass off Nick's furs. "Welcome to Asgard, lad," he said.

Chapter 7

Nick staggered, his head spinning from his sudden trip. "Easy, lad," Baldur said, steadying him with a hand on his arm. "It's always like that the first time."

"What happened?" asked Nick unsteadily.

"We crossed the bridge," replied Baldur.

"It seemed like I went into the rainbow, not over it."

"You did. The Bifrost is the bridge between Midgard and Asgard. You went into the rainbow in Midgard and passed through it to Asgard."

"I thought we'd walk on it," Nick said, looking over Baldur's shoulder at the rainbow.

"How would we climb that?" asked Baldur, pointing at the rainbow arching up into the sky and over the mountains, which were now behind them.

"True," said Nick. His head began to clear. "I wasn't expecting to be teleported though."

"Tele-what?" asked Baldur, scowling.

Nick thought for a moment, then decided that explaining science fiction technology to a Norse warrior would be a little too hard. "Never mind," he said.

Baldur's eyebrows crinkled as he studied Nick. "We entered the bridge at one end and were taken to a far place. In an instant."

"Exactly," said Nick with a smile.

"That's why Heimdall keeps watch. Because once the giants make it to the bridge, they'll be on us in an instant."

"Not with that wolf there," said Nick. He shuddered at the howling, slobbery memory. "Nobody's getting past him."

"You did, lad," Baldur said. He smiled and clapped Nick on the shoulder. "That was well done."

Nick was genuinely pleased at Baldur's praise but also somehow embarrassed. He looked at the ground and mumbled, "Thanks."

"I don't know this Florida you're from, but they make their lads from stern stuff. Floridian steel, I'd say."

Still embarrassed, Nick turned back to the field of golden grass. The long stalks shimmered in the golden sunlight as they rippled in a gentle breeze. "I thought Asgard would be colder," he said. A bird sang from a distant tree. "But it's warm. And quiet."

Everyone knows it's a jinx to say something like that. Especially in an adventure story. This was no exception.

A blast of horns and a wave of shouts ripped across the meadow. Men poured onto the field from every direction, shouting insults and curses that Nick shouldn't have heard, and even worse, shouldn't have understood. There were so many of them and they were moving so fast that Nick couldn't really see any one person. What he did see were swords and axes, leather and shields, beards and braids, and lots of horned helmets.

As the men careened toward each other, Nick instinctively backed into Baldur.

"Don't worry," Baldur said. "They don't usually get this close to the bridge."

"Usually?" asked Nick.

"Sure," said Baldur. "They do this every day."

The men crashed into each other in the center of the field and immediately began bashing each other brains in. The sound was like nothing Nick had ever heard before. Men screamed battle cries, swords clanged off axes, hammers echoed off shields. Then new noises—softer, gurgling, slurpy noises—started as men began to fall.

"No need for you to watch that," said Baldur as he put his hand on Nick's shoulder and turned him away from the gore of the battle. Nick wasn't sorry that Baldur had shielded him but he still felt compelled to watch the men fight. Baldur's hand tightened. "Maybe another time," he said in the classic voice parents use when they're saying "There's no way you're ever doing this but I'll pretend maybe you can someday if you stop doing it now."

"Besides, here's what you want to see," continued Baldur. He firmly kept Nick's back to the battle and pointed.

The western horizon was filled with castles. A great golden castle stood at the center, its gold towers reaching far above the others. Massive gold walls stretched to either side in front of it, broken only by an open, golden gate. Nick had never seen anything like it. Only his dad's space shuttle came close.

"Valhalla," said Baldur. "Odin's home. And our destination. C'mon."

As the two trekked closer, Nick's amazement grew with the castle. It was enormous and gold and glorious. Towers, towers, and more towers rose from a massive central court and Nick couldn't even count the number of windows. He couldn't imagine how many people the castle could hold. "You could never fill it," said Nick in amazement.

Baldur seemed to understand him. "Probably not," he said. "But the Valkyrior will try."

"Valky-who?"

"The Warrior Maidens. The women who choose the bravest warriors to join Odin in Valhalla."

"Did they choose you?" Nick asked.

Baldur looked startled. "No."

"Why not? You're brave."

"Maybe. But I haven't died in battle yet." He saw Nick's confusion. "They gather the spirits of warriors who fight and die bravely."

"Then I hope you're never chosen," Nick said.

Baldur furrowed his eyebrows at Nick, looking a little offended. Then, his face lightened and he explained, "Being chosen is the greatest honor there is, lad. If the Valkyrior bring you to Valhalla, you get to fight all day, be healed, and then feast all night. And when Ragnarok comes, you get to stand with Odin and the other gods against the giants." Baldur looked up at the gleaming golden towers. "There would be nothing better."

Nick didn't quite understand. "But to be chosen you have to die?" he said.

"In battle," agreed Baldur.

"What if you die some other way?" asked Nick.

"Then you go to Niffleheim and live with Hela and everyone else who fell to sickness or accidents or old age."

"Is that a nice place too?"

Baldur stared at Nick. "No, lad. No it isn't." He shook his head, making his red beard wag. "Florida must really be far away."

"That's not right," protested Nick. "How can living a long time be wrong?"

"How long you live isn't the issue. It's how you live."

Nick didn't understand that at all. His expression apparently said so. "Odin needs warriors," said Baldur. "And he only wants those with true courage at his side when it's time to fight the giants."

"So he can beat them." Nick barely noticed the golden grass and trees as they continued toward the castle.

"Oh, we won't win," said Baldur casually.

Nick stopped. "What?"

"We won't win."

"What do you mean?"

Baldur stopped and turned back to Nick. "We'll destroy the giants. Every last one. But they'll destroy us too. If we fight well enough though, one man and one woman will survive and they will recreate the earth."

Nick opened his mouth then closed it then opened it again. Finally, he said, "How can you stand that?"

"Stand what?" asked Baldur

"That you're all going to die."

Baldur shrugged. "Everyone dies. It's up to us to live fully and die well." Baldur stared at Nick a moment longer then waved him forward and started toward the castle again. Nick trotted to catch up. "It's different in your Florida?"

"Got that right."

"You have no battles?"

"All we fight is the heat."

Baldur shook his head. "How boring."

As you might imagine, Nick really didn't like this talk about battles and death, and the thought of Baldur (and everyone else) being destroyed by giants made him uneasy. On top of that, talking about Florida, and its heat, made him homesick. He found himself missing his dad even more.

Baldur saw this as they arrived at the gates to Valhalla. "Enough, lad," Baldur said and put a hand on Nick's shoulder. "Do your best, enjoy what you have, and the rest will take care of itself. Worry just saps your strength and bunges up your bowels." Baldur smiled. "Now let's see what Odin knows about sending you home."

And with that, Nick Snow entered the gates of Valhalla. His only friend in all of Midgard went right along with him.

Nick and Baldur found Odin in his golden hall. When they did, Nick decided that Odin was the strangest, most fearsome man he had ever seen.

Odin sat on a raised golden throne. Two crows were perched on the All-Father's massive shoulders and the sight was so striking and so strange that Nick barely noticed the two wolves sitting at Odin's feet (which, I think you'll agree, was pretty remarkable considering recent events). A shield as big as Nick was propped negligently on one side of the throne. Odin held a spear upright on the other side, its butt resting on the golden floor. His bare arms bulged with the muscles of a young man, although his long beard was snow white. The whiteness of his beard emphasized the blackness of the patch covering his right eye and Nick felt the stare from Odin's single good eye as he approached the throne.

They were barely halfway across the room when Odin boomed, "Baldur, you scruff! Where have you been! I've missed you." And with that, Odin hurled his spear at Baldur.

Nick barked a curse he shouldn't have known (and which we won't report) and leapt to the side. Baldur crossed his arms and smiled as the spear sped straight for his heart. It bounced away and clattered to the floor. "Hello, Father," he said. "I missed you too."

The two gods laughed as Nick scrambled back to his feet. Baldur picked up the spear and steadied Nick with a hand as the two approached the throne. When they got close, the two wolves raised their heads and gave the slightest growl.

"Easy, boys," said Baldur. "I'm just giving it back to him." He tossed the spear to Odin, who caught it with another bark of laughter. Then Baldur bent and scratched one wolf behind the ears. The wolf let him. "This is Freki, lad," said Baldur to Nick. "His brother Geri will let you do the same."

"No thanks," said Nick. "I'm full up on wolves today."

Geri lowered his head, looking slightly offended. For a wolf.

Odin stepped down from the throne and gave his son a rough hug (no easy task with crows on your shoulders). He slapped Baldur's back once before grabbing his arm. "Glad you're back," he growled. "I've had to throw at straw targets while you were gone."

"Thought you seemed a little off there."

Odin's voice was fierce but his eye sparkled. "That throw would have split a kernel of corn from one hundred paces and you know it."

"I don't know. It seemed a little wide to me."

As Odin scoffed and Baldur offered his opinion that Tyr threw better with his handless arm, Nick noticed the obvious gruff affection between father and son. It reminded him of how he felt when he came home and his dad was already there (on days he didn't have to present a math test of course) and made him miss his dad a little more.

"Who's your jumpy friend, Son?" Odin finally asked.

"Father, this is Nick Snow of Florida."

Odin stared at Nick with his one eye, and his look was neither mean nor happy but intense. Though he tried to meet Odin's gaze, Nick's eyes kept straying to the eyepatch. He was afraid he was offending Odin when the crows suddenly turned and whispered in Odin's ears. And I don't mean softly cheeping or squawking either. Nick actually heard the crows whisper words in soft chirping voices. It creeped Nick out.

Odin nodded. "Hugin and Munin say they haven't seen you before," he said. "Which is strange because they see everything. So where is this Florida you've come from? How do you get there?"

Nick was paralyzed. Having a one-eyed god stare at you will do that.

Baldur jumped in. "We're not sure, Father. That's why we're here. To find a way to send him home. We were hoping you could help."

Odin stared from Baldur to Nick to Baldur again. "You'd better tell me the whole story, Son."

So they did. They told Odin how Nick had been given the card game, how his picture had been in it, and how he'd arrived in the snow only to be chased by giants. Nick explained how one of the giants had wanted the cards, how Baldur had saved him and decided to guide him to Odin, and how they'd passed the wolf to come to Asgard. When they finally described how they'd arrived at Odin's throne, Nick and Baldur fell silent. Two wolves, two crows and a god looked back at them skeptically.

"Were it not for the color of your skin, I might not believe you had come so far," said Odin finally. "Does your land really lie beyond the snow?"

"Yes, Mr. Odin," replied Nick. Nick was uncertain how you addressed a god. His dad was big on showing respect for your elders but Nick bet that even James Snow would have to look up the proper title to address Mr. Eyepatch-Wearing-Crow-Listening-All-Father-Lord-of-Asgard-Sir. Mister seemed the safest.

Odin didn't seem to mind. "Let's see these cards then."

Nick reached into his pocket (which was made a little harder by the furs) and pulled out his Norse deck. He shuffled through the cards until he came to the by now familiar red one marked Adventure. He held it out to Odin. Odin reached out to take it.

Hugin and Munin screamed.

Odin started back as the crows screeched and flapped their wings frantically. "I guess I won't take it," said Odin, looking at each shoulder as if his birds were crazy (and as if that were a normal thing to do.) "Just hold it out so I can see it."

Nick obediently held the card up for Odin. Nick tried not to stare at Odin's eyepatch but he couldn't help it; the circle of black stood alone, surrounded by the white of Odin's hair and beard. Nick forced himself to look at Odin's one eye, which was staring intently at the Adventure card. The crows leaned forward as if they were reading too. Odin's eye twitched, flicking back and forth. He began to tap his spear against the floor. His eyebrows bunched. The spear tapped faster. He leaned closer, staring.

Suddenly, Odin slammed the spear butt on the floor. "I can't read it!" he barked.

Nick jumped and the crows flapped and squawked.

"The runes are strange, Father," said Baldur.

"But I invented runes!" replied Odin.

"Apparently not these," said Baldur in the voice of a son who knew how to get his father's goat.

"Watch it, scruff!" said Odin. "Or I'll have your mother make everything take back that promise!"

"Now why would I do that?" came a melodious voice over their shoulders.

Nick turned to face a woman as beautiful as Odin was strange. Like everyone here, she was tall. Thick, blond braids hung almost to her waist and she seemed to glide across the room as her thick green robe trailed behind her. She glided up to Baldur, put a hand on one of his cheeks, and kissed the other one. "Why would I let anything hurt my darling boy?"

Baldur actually blushed. "Mother," he said. "This is Nick Snow of Florida."

"So I've heard," she said, giving Nick the biggest smile he'd received since he'd plopped into Midgard.

"Nick, this is my mother, Frigga."

"Hello, Mrs. Frigga," said Nick, using the same name strategy he'd used with Odin.

"Hello, Nick Snow of Florida," Frigga said seriously. "You are courteous. Which is more than I can say for some." She threw Odin a glance.

"I can't read the runes," Odin said, as if that explained everything.

"Yes?" Frigga replied.

"I invented runes," said Odin.

"Apparently not these," Frigga replied.

Odin snorted. "You're as bad as him."

"Let me see," she said.

"You won't be able to read them," said Odin.

"Of course not," Frigga replied.

Nick held his Adventure Card up to Frigga now. She bent down to look, with Odin peering over her shoulder.

Frigga's blue eyes widened and she snapped upright so fast she knocked Odin's winged helmet sideways. Nick flinched, startled by her reaction. "Hasn't my son been good to you?" Frigga said wildly.

"What?" said Nick.

"What?" said Odin.

"What?" said Baldur.

"Hasn't my son been good to you?" she insisted.

"Sure," said Nick. "He saved my life."

"Then why are you going to kill him?"

Chapter 8

"Mother!" exclaimed Baldur, looking completely embarrassed.

Nick stared at the goddess, utterly unsure what to say. She stared back, waiting. "Mrs. Frigga," he said finally. "I wouldn't hurt him!"

Frigga towered over him. Her disbelief pressed down on Nick. "So you say."

"Why would I do that, Mrs. Frigga?" Nick felt a hot pressure behind his eyes. "He's the only friend I have in this world." Nick clenched his teeth and forced himself not to cry.

"Promise that you will not harm Baldur," Frigga said relentlessly. "Swear like every other thing in the world. Swear by the Midgard Serpent and the great Tree that you will not harm the man who stands before you wearing the silver and ruby armring, that you will not hurt him, and that your hand will always turn aside."

Nick looked from Frigga to Baldur, who stood scowling at his mother with his great arms crossed, the silver and ruby armring shimmering on his left arm. "Say the words," continued Frigga sternly. "I give my oath . . ."

"I give my oath . . ." followed Nick.

"That I will not harm the man who stands before me wearing the silver and ruby armring . . ."

"That I will not harm the man who stands before me wearing the silver and ruby armring . . ."

"That I will not hurt him and that my hand will always turn aside . . ."

"That I will not hurt him and that my hand will always turn aside . . ."

"This I swear by the Midgard Serpent and the great Tree."

"This I swear by the Midgard Serpent and the great Tree," finished Nick, lowering his head. Though he kept the tears out of his eyes, he couldn't hide the hurt on face. "But you didn't have to make me."

Frigga saw it. Or something more. She crouched down and swept him up into a great green-robed hug. "You do care for him, don't you," she said softly.

Nick nodded into her shoulder, unable to speak. She stroked the back of Nick's head.

"You didn't have to do that." said Baldur, scowling.

"Yes, I did," replied Frigga.

"How could you read the card?" asked Odin.

"I couldn't," said Frigga as she continued to soothe Nick. "But I saw the cards in my dream. *The* dream."

Nick's hand began to vibrate. He pulled back from Frigga's shoulder. He'd forgotten that he still held the cards and now the deck was buzzing in his hand. He looked at the blank side of the cards, the three gods huddled around him. As they watched, a picture of a snake eating its tail while wrapped around a globe appeared.

"'The Midgard Serpent'," Nick read.

"That's him," said Odin.

"I still can't read it," said Baldur. "What does it say?"

"Stupid runes," muttered Odin.

Nick read the inscription:

> *The Midgard Serpent grew so large it encircled the world, holding its tail in its mouth. Add 10 to its attack if its father Loki is on the field.*

Frigga stared at the card. "Has this happened before?" she asked.

"Twice," answered Nick.

"Who appeared?" she asked.

"You. And Odin. Here," Nick showed them their cards.

"I am one striking man," said Odin appreciatively.

"Hush," said Frigga. "How did it happen?"

"When you said the names, lad," blurted Baldur. "It happened when you said their names. And just now, when you said 'Midgard Serpent.'"

"Say Baldur's name," said Frigga seriously.

"What?" replied Nick, a little confused.

"Say Baldur's name."

Nick shrugged and held up a blank card. "Baldur," he said. They waited. Nothing.

"Baldur," Nick said again. The card stayed blank. "Maybe that's not how it works," he said.

The crows whispered in Odin's ear. "Sure," he said. "Try them, Snow. Say Hugin and Munin."

Nick held up the cards. "Hugin," he said. "Munin."

They waited again. Then the deck began to vibrate. On two different cards, a crow appeared. One was labeled Hugin, the other Munin.

"Well look at that," said Baldur. "You can see both of . . ."

"Say Baldur again," interrupted Frigga. Nick looked a question at her. "Please," she said.

Nick held up another card. "Baldur."

Nothing.

"He must not be one of the cards," suggested Nick.

"Let him quit mother," said Baldur. They could all see the strange look on Frigga's face. "What is it, Mother?"

"I told you," she replied. "These cards were in the dream."

"So?" asked Baldur.

"The cards were in Niffleheim," she said softly. She looked up at Baldur. "So were you."

Nick remembered what Baldur had told him about Niffleheim, the cold, dark place where the old and the sick and the cowards went after they died. Although Nick still didn't see anything wrong with being old or sick, he remembered how serious Baldur had been about it. He also remembered that those who went there wouldn't get to live with Odin in Valhalla or fight with him at Ragnarok.

Baldur's face turned that pale white-green that people get right before they barf. It looked like he remembered too.

"I'm not going to do anything," Nick said again, to Baldur this time.

"I know, lad," Baldur said with a smile.

"I believe him too," said Frigga in a mostly-convinced voice. "But we need to help him, and his cards, find a way home. Now. The sooner they leave Midgard, the better."

"Well it's not going to happen before dinner," said Odin. "What?" he said in answer to Frigga's look. "I can't read his cards, and I don't know where this 'Florida' is, so I don't even know where we're finding a way back to yet. We'll go to the feast first, then figure it out."

Frigga looked at him skeptically. "These things take time," Odin said with a shrug. "Besides, the lads have got to be hungry. Right boys?"

How can you refuse an invitation from a crow-wearing god? Besides, Nick found that he was suddenly starving. He realized that, although he'd almost been a meal several times today, he hadn't eaten one. Nick nodded his agreement. Baldur joined him. Hugin (or maybe Munin) squawked.

"Great," said Odin. "The feast just started. Let's eat."

"And then you'll help young Snow find a way home?" Frigga's intensity returned.

"Of course." Odin turned to Nick. "So how do you like your boar?"

Five minutes later, the four of them (six counting crows), arrived at a pair of golden doors at least fifty feet high. A crow flying over a rainbow was carved in the center. Nick barely had time to study them before Odin said, "Stand back when Baldur goes in, Nick Snow. People get a little excited to see him."

Nick nodded. With a grin, Odin pushed open the great doors as if they were light as cardboard and Baldur strode into the feast hall.

There was a pause and then a great cry rose from the hall. "Baldur!" they all shouted. There was a great clatter and scrape as a hall full of men rose to their feet and, a second later, weapons of all shapes and sizes went airborne, hurtling straight toward Baldur. He didn't move.

Odin quickly ducked back and shut the doors in front of him. Hugin and Munin flapped their wings as the weapons crashed into the thick wood. Odin smiled down at Nick as the doors shook with the impact of spears, hammers, and gods knew what else. "How can you not chuck a weapon at an invincible friend?" he said. "It's irresistible." There was a crash like a boulder hitting the wall and the handles shook in Odin's hands. "It's a little dangerous to stand near him though."

"I noticed," said Nick as the doors still trembled.

When the clatter died down, Odin reopened the doors. He pushed through a pile of axes and arrows, swords and daggers, tankards, cups, and plates, and even large bones (mostly ribs by the look of them). Baldur stood in the middle of them, smiling. "Evening, lads," he said.

A general cry of welcome went up with many "Ho Baldur's," "Hail Odin's," and "Good Frigga's" rising to meet them as they stepped into the hall. As Nick picked his way over the wreckage of Baldur's welcome, he finally got a look at the feast.

The hall was light and gold and warm. A long table extended almost as far as Nick could see. A great boar turned on a spit on one side of the hall. Towering men and women dressed in leather armor milled everywhere, wandering from the boar to a row of casks where they helped themselves to drinks by dipping large horns into the wooden barrels. Those at the table slapped their meat onto great circles of bread and washed it down with huge gulps from their horns. Each bite seemed to be punctuated with a shout and each drink with a yell. Laughter came from everywhere.

As they walked to the head of the table, many of the feasters wandered up to slap Baldur's shoulder or to compliment Odin on the feast. Only a few approached Frigga and when they did, they were quiet and courteous. No one said anything to Nick, but a great many stared.

"Time for a bit of a show," said Odin to Nick with a wink of his one eye. He snatched a horn from a man's hand, ignoring the man's surprised expression. "Hail, heroes!" he bellowed down the table.

"Odin!" the heroes cried.

"I see you're all eating my eternal boar."

A chorus of You betcha's, Absotootley's and Darn Tootin's arose.

"Did you at least fight today?"

"Always," came the cried reply.

"Each day you fight in my field," said Odin. "Each afternoon, you are healed and return to my hall. Each night, you
eat the boar Schrimnir. And each morning, the boar becomes
whole so we can do it all again. Eat! Be renewed! And tomorrow go and fight again that your strength may grow and that
we may vanquish the giants when Heimdall sounds his horn!
May it be soon!"

"Soon!" the heroes cried and broke into cheers as Odin
raised his horn, then drained it.

Odin returned to Nick. "That should give us some peace
for a bit," he said. And sure enough, the heroes went back to
their wandering feast, and left them alone.

"Here, sit," said Odin as a place at the head of the table and
seats alongside quickly cleared. Nick took a place between
Odin and Baldur. Nick saw no servants but before he knew
it, men had placed bread and horns and haunches of boar on
the table. Nick had never been a big fan of pork but the
steaming meat and sizzling fat had his mouth watering and
before he knew it, he was chin deep in ribs, the juice drip-
ping from his mouth and fingers. Nick was starving, and he
gobbled his boar faster than his grandma's turkey.

Thinking of his grandma made him remember his manners.
He looked for a napkin but there was nothing of the kind. He
watched as Baldur sopped up the grease with a hunk of bread
and ate it. "Cool," Nick said. And did the same.

Nick devoted his full attention to eating. He felt as if he
hadn't eaten in weeks and he tore into his food with the gusto

of a Norse hero. The bread was warm and filling and the boar was seasoned like nothing he'd ever tasted. For a solid half hour, Nick didn't think about trying to get home or talking to the gods. In fact, he barely even realized that he was sitting in Valhalla eating with three gods and a hall full of heroes (which should make you realize just how hungry, and adaptable, Nick was). No, Nick just ate until he was stuffed.

The only distraction to his eating was the projectiles. Every so often, an ax would come flying toward Baldur. Baldur ignored it of course but Nick had to keep ducking behind Odin's shield before an ax (or arrow or hammer) bashed his skull in. Fortunately, Odin was ready, quick, and fairly understanding (for a mean-looking, one-eyed god). In fact, he seemed to get a kick out of it, chuckling every time something bounced off his son and laughing outright when he shielded Nick.

"What the heck was that?" yelped Nick, peaking around Odin's shield after a particularly loud clang.

"A shovel," said Baldur, without looking.

"A shovel?" asked Nick. "Now they're throwing garden tools? This is crazy!"

"Actually, they're being pretty respectful," said Baldur as he finished his meal.

"Respectful? They haven't stopped chucking stuff at you since we walked in!"

"Yeah, but none of it's squishy. Nobody wants to offend Odin or Frigga by splashing them."

"Squishy?"

"Pies. Chickens. Pig bladders."

"Pig bladders?"

"Yeah. They fill them up with water 'till they're big as a melon, tie the end, and toss it. It soaks whatever it hits when it breaks."

Nick began to see where Baldur's patience came from. "Isn't it annoying?" asked Nick.

"A little," admitted Baldur.

"It's better than the alternative," said Frigga from the other side of the table. "Now finish your boar."

"Yes, ma'am," Nick and Baldur said in unison.

"Ah, there's good boys," said a red-haired man who stood at the table. He smirked as he took a seat next to Baldur. "You should always listen to your mommy."

"No giants to eat with in Jotunheim, Loki?" said Baldur not looking up from his plate. "Or do your half-brothers find your company as enjoyable as we do?"

"You know nothing compares to Odin's feast, Baldur," said Loki smoothly. "And if anyone is keeping strange company these days, it's you."

Nick felt heat rise to his face at the insult. Loki sat there smirking. His green eyes glittered mischievously in a way Nick thought was familiar. Nick didn't know who Loki reminded him of but he knew they hadn't met. His beardless, smart aleck face was too distinctive to forget. Nick instantly disliked him.

Baldur turned and faced Loki, bearing down on him with his full attention. "I know you're not insulting my friend."

"Of course not," said Loki, who kept smirking but also leaned back a bit.

"Especially when he's eating at my father's table."

"No, that would be rude."

"So rude I'd be obliged to do something about it." As if for emphasis, a spear came arcing across the room. It bounced off Baldur and clattered to the floor.

"We wouldn't want that," said Loki, his eyes following the spear.

"No, we wouldn't." Baldur returned his attention to his food. "Nick Snow, this is Loki. Don't trust him."

"Hello, Mr. Loki," said Nick politely.

"Welcome to Asgard, Nick Snow," said Loki without taking his eyes off Baldur. "Baldur and I have known each other for a long time. I hope you didn't think I was talking about you."

"Don't believe him either," said Baldur.

Nick's pocket began to vibrate. Nick put his hand over it, trying to muffle the sound.

Loki's looked directly at Nick for the first time, green eyes glittering. He glanced briefly at Nick's hand before shaking his head and continuing, "I don't know what I've ever done to deserve such mistrust." Loki would have seemed sad if he weren't still smirking.

"Ask Thor," said Baldur, taking another bite of boar.

"A misunderstanding. Besides, I've never done anything to you."

"Only because you can't."

"Baldur," Loki said. "Your mother's oath was hardly necessary with me. You underestimate my good nature. I for one am grateful for the true extent of your mother's love." Baldur just stared at him.

Loki sighed. "Misunderstood again. Well, I have no wish to upset any of you so I'll move on down the table. Odin, Frigga," he nodded to each. "A wonderful feast as always. Nick Snow," he looked Nick up and down. "My pup said you were brave. I hope we meet again. Soon." Then he rose and sauntered down toward the other end of the table.

"I don't know why you put up with him," Frigga said to Odin.

"He's useful," said Odin.

"He's annoying," said Frigga. "Walking around here smirking all the time and up to no good more often than not. And those children of his," Frigga shuddered. "How can you trust a man who sires a wolf and a serpent."

"Don't forget Hela," said Baldur.

"And Hela," said Frigga, nodding. "The most normal looking of the three but deep down, the worst. You just can't trust a man like that."

"I never said I trusted him," Odin replied. "I said he was useful. And he is."

Frigga shook her head. "You'll regret that use one day."

"I'll keep an eye on him," replied Odin seriously, tapping his eyepatch.

Nick and Baldur laughed. Odin didn't seem to mind.

With a ping, ping, ping, three rocks came whizzing by Nick and bounced off Baldur. "Hold still," yelled someone down the table. Those in between started to laugh. "Yeah, hold still," they cried.

Baldur gave Nick a small grin. "They won't stop 'till I do you know."

"You're excused," Nick grinned back.

"Thanks," Baldur said and stood. "I'll be right back." He turned and faced the crowd, giving the men a mocking bow. Then he held his arms out to the sides and said, "What are you, blind? I'm standing right here!"

Hoots and hollers rose from around the table as a storm of weapons descended. Arrows, spears, and stones fell on Baldur like rain and bounced off as harmlessly. One after another, the projectiles turned away, bound by their promise not to harm him. Eventually, the flurry stopped and the yells lessened, not because the men were having less fun, but because they were running out of things to throw. Baldur stood there patiently, arms outstretched, the red stone of his armring flashing in the light. Though he had seemed reluctant to stand, he was grinning.

"Better luck next time, lads." Baldur said. "Work on your aim. The lot of you couldn't hit a barn wall from the inside." He laughingly turned back to Nick and made to sit down.

As the noise lessened, Nick heard a grunt and then the faint whoosh of another missile. Baldur didn't even bother to turn as

Nick saw a strange spear arc toward Baldur. Rather than a metal head, the pointed end of this one looked like a sharpened stick. The back end had a bunch of green puffing out from the shaft. Nick thought at first that the green puff was feathers, but as the strange spear approached, Nick saw they were leaves.

A scream burst from across the table, a horrible rising scream that sounded like a wildcat. Startled, Nick and Baldur both jumped and turned. It was Frigga. As the spear descended toward Baldur, Nick thought he caught the word she screeched—"Mistletoe!" Nick whirled back in time to see the strange, leafy spear plummet straight towards Baldur.

Unlike the others though, this one didn't veer.

Before he could speak or move or even duck, the spear plunged into Baldur's side. He staggered and grabbed at the table. His hands slipped off the wood like it was coated in grease. He stumbled, then fell to the floor. The shaft of the spear stuck out of the side of his chest, the ball of sharp green leaves at the end trembling with each ragged breath.

Nick leapt from his seat down to Baldur's side. Baldur's eyes flickered open for a moment. "That stings a bit," he said with a faint smile. "Trust Odin, lad. He'll help you." Then Baldur closed his eyes and went still.

Frigga's scream turned into a raw, keening wail that Nick never forgot. Nick stared at his big friend for a moment, uncertain what had happened. Then he knew.

Baldur was dead.

Chapter 9

"It was so small," cried Frigga. She held Baldur's head in her lap, stroking his hair over and over. "It was so small."

Nick sat beside her, holding Baldur's hand. He wasn't sure what hurt him more, Frigga's tears or Baldur's cold skin. "What was so small, Mrs. Frigga?" he asked quietly.

"I didn't think it could hurt him," Frigga insisted. "It was too small."

"What was too small?" Nick repeated.

"The mistletoe," she said. "It was such a tiny plant. I didn't think it could hurt him."

"It's okay, Mrs. Frigga," Nick said. "It's not your fault."

"It is my fault!" cried Frigga and Nick watched helplessly as tears streamed down the beautiful goddess's cheeks. "I knew! I went to everything in the world and made them promise. Everything! Except the mistletoe. I didn't go to the mistletoe."

Frigga stopped. Tears dropped from her cheeks and glistened like crystals on Odin's stone floor. She stroked Baldur's hair and when she spoke again, it was in a whisper. "I didn't ask the mistletoe. It was the only thing. Such a small and scrawny thing. Nothing so small could ever harm my son, a god." Frigga shook her head over and over. "The only thing in all the world that didn't promise. The only thing. And it killed him. I killed him."

Nick had never seen such raw pain and guilt and grief in his whole short life, especially from an adult. He couldn't stand it. "You couldn't have known," he said, trying his best to make Frigga feel better.

"I'm his mother," she replied. "I have to know."

"You made almost everything promise not to hurt him. It's amazing. You couldn't have done anything more."

"I could have," she whispered. "And because I failed, he's dead. My good Baldur is dead."

"You are not the reason my son is dead," boomed Odin. Nick jumped as the All-Father's voice cracked like a gravelly thunderclap and turned to see Odin towering over them. Where Frigga's eyes welled with tears, Odin's eye blazed with an anger that threatened to burn everything around them. "You didn't throw that spear," he growled. He raised his eye to the hall. "But I want the man who did."

A gap opened in the heroes of the hall as if Odin's eye were cutting a path. A murmur rose and Nick soon saw that the heroes pushed a man forward toward Odin. Whispers of "murderer" and "slayer" followed the man as he came. He wore a tattered brown robe and his long brown hair straggled over his eyes. He bounced from side to side as the heroes pushed him, staggering as if he were having trouble keeping his balance, as if he were unprepared for each push.

The tattered man held a sharpened stick in one hand. A tuft of sharp green leaves sprouted from the other end.

Frigga hissed sharply when she saw the spear that matched the one sticking out of her son's side. "Look what he holds!" she hissed. "Strike him down, Odin!"

Odin didn't move.

Odin's silence infuriated Frigga. "Look at him!" hissed Frigga. "Look what he holds! Why do you wait? Destroy him!"

"Yes, Frigga," said Odin, crossing his arms. "Look at him."

Frigga swiveled from Odin to the man to Odin, puzzled.

"Look at him, wife," Odin said gently. "Look who it is."

The tattered man lifted his straggly brown head to Frigga and Nick. His eyes were a solid, milky white.

He was blind.

"What has happened, All-Father?" the man whispered. He was trembling.

"My son is slain, Hador," said Odin bluntly. "By a spear from your hand."

Hador's face turned as white as his eyes and he shook even more. "But how All-Father? Baldur can't be harmed by anything in Asgard."

"Nothing except mistletoe. Which you carry."

Hador dropped the other spear. The clatter echoed like a cymbal in the silent hall. "I didn't know."

"Perhaps," said Odin. "How did you come by the spear?"

"It was given to me," said Hador.

"You'll need to do better than that," said Odin, his eye a beam of concentrated menace.

Hador couldn't see that menace, but he obviously felt it and trembled even more, his hands fidgeting inside the fringes of his tattered, brown cloak. "I was eating at the far end of the table when Baldur entered your hall. I heard the shouts that greeted your son, the whizzing of weapons toward him, the clatter of wood on stone as they missed, and the shared laughter of friendship. The story of your son is well-known." Hador stopped, his blind eyes twitching from side to side as if trying to see the threat to him. Odin said nothing and waited.

"I wanted to join in," whispered Hador.

"Why?" said Odin.

"For the same reason everyone else does. It's fun."

When Odin fell silent again, Hador continued. "Everyone went back to eating but all spoke of their throws—how far they went, how close they came, how everything turned away at the last moment. When we'd eaten, I felt the air move with the flight of more weapons and heard someone yell 'Hold still.' Then I heard Baldur say, 'What are you blind? I'm standing right here.'" Hador shook his straggly head.

"After that, a voice next to me said, 'Would you have a turn brother? He seems to be calling you.'"

"'I would, friend,' I replied, 'if you would guide my hand.'"

"'Of course,' said the voice. A hand on my elbow guided me up and to one side of the table. The smooth shaft of a spear was pressed into my hand. Then someone grasped my shoulders, turned me, and said, 'That way. Hurry, while he still stands.' And I hurled the spear with all my strength."

Hador rubbed his hands under his tattered cloak and blinked his sightless eyes. "I laughed along with the rest and the voice laughed with me. 'Did it work?' I asked."

"'Oh yes,' the voice replied. Then the room fell quiet and I heard Frigga's scream."

Hador fell to his knees, his blind eyes staring at the stone floor. "All-Father, forgive me. Please. I would never seek to harm Baldur the Good. I didn't know."

Hugin turned his head and whispered in Odin's ear. "I will never forgive you, Hador," replied Odin. "But I will spare you. The hand was yours. The plot was not." Munin now whispered in Odin's other ear. The All-Father shook his head. "But I cannot yet tell whose it was."

"Odin!" interrupted Frigga, her face suddenly panicked. She quickly ran one hand along Baldur's bare arm, then furiously patted his vest, as if looking for something. "That must wait. Summon the Valkyrior. Save his spirit."

Odin stared at her for a moment. It seemed to Nick that kindness radiated from that one eye. "Frigga," Odin said gently.

"Summon them!" yelled Frigga.

Odin opened his mouth to speak, then stopped and shook his head. "Okay," he said with a sigh.

Nick didn't see or hear Odin do anything. But moments later, there was a sound like trumpets and beams of light streamed down from the ceiling. Three women glided down the light to the floor. Winged helmets covered their streaming blond hair. Each woman carried a gleaming spear and a shining shield that reflected the light as they walked to Baldur. Nick's jaw dropped as the three women glided up to him. They looked beautiful and dangerous and otherworldly.

He unconsciously dropped Baldur's hand and backed up a step, knowing instinctively that they had come for Baldur. Frigga didn't move. She just sat holding Baldur's head in her lap as the first of the women bent down and touched Baldur's chest. The Valkyrie waited only a moment before she stood. She looked at Odin, shook her head, and turned back toward the light. Her two companions turned with her.

"No," yelled Frigga again. "He must stay."

The Valkyrior ignored her. They walked back to the light, glided up it, and disappeared.

"No," Frigga yelled again. "You can't let them go. He must stay. They must keep his spirit here, in Valhalla. With you," Frigga trailed off. "With me."

"It's too late," said Odin. He spoke gently, like he was holding a delicate glass plate he was afraid to break. "His spirit is gone."

"But it should be here," said Frigga, almost pleading. "He died in battle."

"No," said Odin, shaking his head sadly. "He died in play. By accident. His soul is not mine."

Nick could see Odin didn't want to say it. He could also see that Frigga wouldn't believe it unless Odin did. So Odin said, "It has already gone."

"To Niffleheim."

The worst part is, Frigga didn't scream. Her mouth worked like she was screaming, but no sound came out. Only tears poured out of her as she rocked back and forth holding her son's head, rubbing his bare arm over and over.

Nick couldn't stand it. She was the only person who had really comforted him while he was here. He remembered the warmth of her hug and the calm, it'll-be-okay feeling it gave him when the pain of being away from home had been too much. He could do no less in return.

Nick reached out to Frigga, supreme goddess of Asgard, and took her hand. She resisted for a moment and tried to keep rubbing Baldur's bare arm. Nick clasped her hand firmly and gently stopped her. He remembered when Baldur first told him about his mother and her promise. "The morning we met," Nick said quietly. "Baldur told me how much you loved him."

Frigga gasped. She took Nick's hand in both of her own and pressed it to her face. He could feel her jaw move silently for a moment longer as she slowly rocked back and forth. Then she slumped over and started to sob.

Frigga clung to Nick's hand as she wept. Nick held on and saw his tears splash with hers onto the cold stone floor. After a moment, he looked up at Odin, who stood above them with his arms crossed, a crow on each shoulder. Though his stance was fierce, Odin's stare was not. "Thank you," Odin mouthed silently. And wiped a tear from his only eye.

"You can save him," said Frigga suddenly. She whipped her head around and stared at Nick with wild eyes.

"What?" said Nick with a start.

"You can bring them back," said Frigga.

"How?"

"I saw your cards with Baldur in Niffleheim. I thought it meant you'd kill him, that you'd send him there. But you didn't. So it must mean that you'll bring him back."

Nick cocked his head, trying to follow the suddenly wild goddess. Finally, he shook his head and said, "What are you talking about?"

"I dreamt that Baldur was in Niffleheim and I dreamt that your cards were there with him," said Frigga slowly as if it were the most obvious thing in the world. "I assumed that meant that you and your cards would kill him. It didn't. It means you're going to bring him back." Her eyes sparkled at the idea.

"How am I going to do that?" asked Nick. Nick didn't know how he could bring Baldur back from Niffleheim (or wherever he was) and the crazy look in Frigga's eyes didn't make him feel any better about it.

"Hela rules Niffleheim. You'll just have to convince her to release him."

"How am I going to do that?" repeated Nick.

Frigga thought for a moment. "The cards. There must be a reason I dreamt about your cards. Look at them again. Quickly! We don't have much time before his spirit is lost to us."

Nick pulled out his Norse deck. He saw Odin and Frigga, Hunin and Munin. There was a fifth card now—a picture of a red-haired man standing before a rainbow with gods on one side and giants on the other. Loki. Nick remembered the deck buzzing when he met the god during dinner and how he had tried to muffle the noise. The card must have appeared then, when he had said the god of mischief's name.

But that didn't help him now. He stared at the cards, thinking, trying to figure out what to do. The hall was quiet, except for Hador, who apparently didn't believe that he wasn't going to be vaporized by Odin. "Please, I didn't know," he mumbled as he still knelt before Odin. "I didn't know anything could hurt Baldur the Good. Please forgive . . ."

"Get him out of here," Odin snapped, waving one hand at the kneeling blind man. "I can't bear to hear him say my son's name."

Suddenly, Nick knew what to do. "Baldur the Good," he said and held up a blank card.

A moment later, the deck began to vibrate.

Nick watched as a picture of Baldur appeared. He was kneeling down holding a spear and stones were bouncing off him. In the upper left corner it said "Baldur the Good."

"Got it!" he said.

"Read it. What does it say?" said Frigga, straining forward. Nick read the inscription aloud to the others:

Frigga made all living things swear never to harm Baldur, except the small and harmless mistletoe. While the gods threw stones at Baldur to watch them bounce off, Loki tricked a blind man into throwing mistletoe which killed him. Baldur cannot be harmed by monsters or minions.

"Find him!" roared Odin. "Bring Loki here! Now!" There was a clatter of metal and arms as dozens of men sprinted out of the hall. "That's one mystery solved," said Odin. "We know who did it but it doesn't bring my son back." Odin's eye burned with an excitement that matched Frigga's madness. "Frigga's right. You must go to Niffleheim."

Another little detail popped into Nick's head. "Isn't Niffleheim for dead people?" he asked.

"Yes," Odin said.

Nick scowled. "How do you plan on sending me there?"

Odin barked a gravelly laugh. "Don't worry, lad. On my horse, of course. He'll take you."

Nick felt relieved. He didn't really think they'd kill him to send him after Baldur but it had been a long day so the thought had occurred to him. With the immediate fear of being killed removed, Nick thought of other ones. Of the dark. Of the cold.

Of the dead.

"By myself?" he asked, dreading the answer.

Odin smiled. "Though you are brave young Snow, I won't send you alone. You must get there quickly if you are to have any chance of bringing Baldur back, but all the speed in Asgard won't help if you get lost on the way. So I will send two companions with you on your journey—my horse, to carry you, and my swiftest son, to guide you."

Nick exhaled (he hadn't even realized he'd been holding his breath) and felt relieved. Well, as relieved as you could be when you've just been charged with bringing a dead guy back from the underworld. But he wouldn't be alone anyway. A horse and a son of Odin should help. And even if they didn't, he'd at least have someone to scream with.

Frigga came closer and crouched in front of Nick. She grabbed his wrists and squeezed every word as she spoke. "You come from a land of sun, where it never snows. If you fail, my son will be trapped forever in a land of darkness and ice."

Frigga put one hand on Nick's cheek. "Though you looked strange to me at first, I see now that your skin has been kissed by the warmth of the sun. That heat will stand you in good stead where you must travel. Go, Sun Warrior. Get my son. Bring him back to the light."

Nick started to say I'll try but stopped when he saw Frigga's eyes. "I will," he said instead.

Then Frigga smiled. And Nick found that he wanted to do everything he could to make her smile again.

Chapter 10

Nick squinted into the bright sun as he left the halls of Valhalla. With Odin and Frigga right behind him, he passed through the golden gates of the castle into the golden fields of Asgard. He lifted his face to the sun, which he'd barely seen since he arrived, and welcomed its warmth as he stopped to take a breath.

Once Nick had agreed to go after Baldur, they'd rushed down to the gates, stopping only to outfit Nick with warmer clothes and better equipment for his journey. Nick now wore calf high, black leather boots with the tops turned down. An oversized black wool shirt hung over thick black pants, gathered around his waist with a silver belt. A silver dagger in a black sheath hung from the belt (just in case, Odin had said). And over it all, a black fur cloak with a deep hood to protect him against the cold.

Nick pulled his fur-lined gloves farther up his wrist and flexed his hand. The strange black clothes made him feel like a hero out of a video game. The Panther, he thought, trying out nicknames. Or Nightfall. Or the Wraith.

How about the Skunk? he could almost hear Chris say. Or maybe the Guinea Pig. Nick grinned at the thought of his friend and shook his head. He wished again Chris could see this because he was never going to believe it.

The thought of his old friend brought Nick back to his quest to save his new one. Odin and Frigga stopped as they reached the edge of the high, golden grass. They looked at Nick as if he knew what to do. He, of course, had no stinking idea.

"The way to Niffleheim is dark and long," said Odin finally. "As I said, you won't go alone. My horse will carry you and my swiftest son will show you the way." Odin put two fingers to his mouth and whistled. His eye crinkled mischievously. "And by swiftest, I mean the fastest."

Nick looked a question at him (showing just how quickly a kid who doesn't know any better can get familiar with the ruler of the gods). "You'll see," Odin said, his mouth curling in a half smile. One of the crows cawed in his ear. "He'll have to see it to believe it," Odin said to the crow. "You're the one who's supposed to see everything, Munin. You should know that." Munin didn't look convinced.

A rumble kept Nick from asking Odin any more questions. It started low, like thunder a long way off on a warm night, but it grew, and grew, and grew, until the pounding waves of noise were almost on top of them. As the noise hit them, Nick thought it sounded like a herd of horses.

It was just one.

A monstrous horse crested a hill and galloped toward them through the golden field. A cloud of grass and dust rose behind it like smoke. Though it was huge, its size alone didn't account for all the racket. It wasn't until the horse broke free of the long grass that Nick saw the reason.

The horse had eight legs. And every one was pounding towards them.

"Sleipnir," said Odin, putting a hand on Nick's shoulder. "Isn't he grand?"

Sure, Nick thought. In an octopus meets Kentucky Derby sort of way. Figuring that wasn't a good answer, Nick just nodded.

The great horse skidded to a stop in front of Odin with the clattering racket of an entire team. Unable to help himself, Nick ducked back behind Odin as the massive steed came to a steaming, spattering halt. Sleipnir dwarfed even Odin, towering over him by at least a head. His pale coat glistened in the sun and his mane was so long it reached to his flanks. As he stamped impatiently (with five of his hooves), his deep muscles rippled and flexed.

Odin patted the horse's neck and affectionately scratched behind his jaw. "Nick Snow this is Sleipnir," said Odin formally. "Sleipnir, this is Nick Snow, the Sun Warrior who is going with you to bring back my son. Do what he asks."

Sleipnir tossed his mane and Nick swore later that the horse actually bowed his head slightly in hello. His hooves tapped a staccato greeting—clip, clip, clop, clip, clop.

"He can bear any load, travel any distance," said Odin proudly to Nick. Sleipnir snorted agreement. "Which will serve you and my son well on this quest." Odin looked around. "If I can find the flaky little good for nothing."

Nick looked another question at Odin. Fortunately, Odin didn't seem offended. "I said you'll see," Odin replied.

"There he is," said Frigga, pointing out over the field.

Nick shaded his eyes and saw a cloud only slightly smaller than Sleipnir's had been a moment before. This time, though, it was being kicked up by a man. Where Sleipnir had plowed through the grass like a thundering wave, this man sliced through the golden stalks with silent swiftness. Before Nick really had time to watch him run, the man stood before them. Like everyone else Nick had met here, he was big. His white blond hair was tied off in braids and so was his long forked beard. He had a shield strapped to his back and carried a large ax in one hand. Though he had run almost as fast as Sleipnir, he was barely breathing hard. Until he started talking anyway.

"Sorry I'm late Father," the man said. "But I was back with the men practicing for tomorrow morning's battle when I got your message that you wanted me and I was going to leave right away but then I had to tend my horse and put away my good armor and before I knew it I was late so I set right out to find you but of course I had to go around the lake and . . ."

"Hermod," said Odin, raising one hand. "This is Nick Snow. You're taking him to Niffleheim. Together, you'll bring Baldur back."

"Of course, Father," said Hermod, nodding. "I was at the feast you know and saw the whole thing. Well I didn't see it exactly because I was throwing axes and then I ran out of axes so I started throwing stones and I ran out of those pretty quick so I was just picking up a cup . . ."

"Hermod," growled Odin.

Hermod's face fell. "Sorry, Father. I mean I was there. I saw what happened to Baldur. I'm sorry."

"Don't be sorry," growled Odin again. "Just get him." Odin and his crows turned to Nick. "This is my son, Hermod. Though he is excitable, and talks too much," Odin threw Hermod a one-eyed glare, "he is faster than all men and most beasts." Sleipnir snorted. "Present company excepted of course. You'll need speed more than anything else. You've got to get to Niffleheim before Hela becomes too attached to Baldur. Hermod and Sleipnir are your best hope."

Hermod stuck out his hand and Nick took it, his small hand engulfed by Hermod's huge one. "Snow, eh?" said Hermod with a smile. "That's a funny name because I hear there's no snow where you're from so how could you be named for snow when there is no snow although I can't believe you never get any snow because everyone knows that even south of here snow falls every wint. . . ."

"Hermod!" snapped Odin.

"Sorry," Hermod dropped his head again. "I mean, nice to meet you, Nick Snow."

"Mount up," said Odin to Hermod. Hermod nodded once and sprang up onto Sleipnir's back. Nick's eyes about fell out of his head at a leap that would probably be a world record high jump at home.

Odin grabbed Nick under each armpit and, easy as you please, dropped him onto Sleipnir's back in front of Hermod.

The ground seemed a ways down and Nick felt dizzy for a second. But then Frigga put a hand on his leg and smiled and everything seemed okay.

"When you get to Niffleheim, go straight to Hela's castle," Frigga said. "Tell her that we will pay any ransom, that we will do whatever she asks, to have Baldur back. Then return and tell us what we must do."

"I will," said Nick, with no idea how he would.

Frigga smiled, just a little. "I know you will, Sun Warrior," she said. "Bring him back to me." She looked at Hermod. "Guide him well. And ward him."

"I will," said Hermod.

"And you," said Odin to Sleipnir. "You've got the most brains in the group. Use them."

Clip-clip, Clop-clop, stomped Sleipnir.

"Then go," said Odin. "And return when your quest is done." Odin leaned in to Nick. "You may want to do the talking when you get there," he whispered. "Hermod's fast, but sometimes his mouth moves faster than his brain."

Nick's eyes widened. He couldn't see himself talking to the goddess of the underworld. He also couldn't see himself refusing Odin, so he just stammered, "Y-Yes, sir."

"Good, Young Snow. I'll count on it." Then Odin straightened and smiled a mischievous grin. "Hie!" he yelled and slapped Sleipnir's flanks.

They took off like a shot.

In a blink, Sleipnir carried them back to the Bifrost bridge and, before Nick even realized what was happening, they galloped into the red of the rainbow bridge and crossed to the other side. Fenris Wolf was waiting but Sleipnir sped past him in one eight-legged stride before the wolf could so much as snap his jaws.

Once they reached Midgard, Sleipnir went even faster. Snow covered trees and fields whizzed past too quickly for Nick to see more than white streaks. The swift wind made by Sleipnir's speed stung Nick's eyes and sent tears streaming down his cheeks. The snow and his watering eyes made the woods they passed, the streams they crossed, and the hills they climbed seem like a constant wet, white blur.

As fast as they were going, Nick knew he should have been scared. But he wasn't. The giant had scared him, Fenris Wolf had scared him, Odin had scared him (at first), Loki had sort of scared him, and the thought of going to the underworld had certainly scared him (and still did). But for some reason, riding an eight-legged horse that was galloping faster than any car didn't bother him in the least. Somehow, of all the things that had happened to him, going incredibly fast didn't seem so strange. It was just fast.

They had ridden (or in Sleipnir's case run) like this for several hours when Hermod reined Sleipnir to a halt in front of a clear stream. "We've only got an hour or so of daylight left," said Hermod. "We'll want to enjoy it."

Nick didn't like the sound of that but started to get off anyway. Then he looked down at the ground, way down at the ground, and decided he could wait.

"Hang on, Nick," said Hermod. He leapt to the ground, landing easily. Then he turned back and grabbed Nick under the armpits just like his father had done. "Some people are afraid of heights," he said as he lifted Nick off Sleipnir's back, "but I never was. Why once when I was only three I climbed to the top of the rainbow quick as you please and there was my mom looking everywhere, combing Asgard for me, and I just sat up there at the top laughing and laughing because I knew she'd never find me unless I . . ."

"Uh, Hermod," interrupted Nick, still hanging in mid-air. Hermod stopped talking and cocked his head to the side. "Could you put me down please?"

Hermod ducked his head sheepishly. "Sure Nick, sorry." He set Nick gently on the ground. "My dad says my brain stops when my mouth starts. Sorry."

"It's okay," said Nick. He took a quick look around in the fading light. They had come to the base of a snow-covered range of hills. Though the snow around them was deep, the stream hadn't iced over and Sleipnir lowered his head for a drink. "Where are we?" Nick asked.

"In Midgard, near the third root of the great tree Ygdrasill that holds up the world with branches that stretch . . ."

Sleipnir snorted and shook his pale mane. Hermod stopped, lowered his head, and sighed. "We're at the beginning of the path that leads down to Niffleheim." Hermod made a face like he was trying to control himself and continued. "The sun's about to set. It's the last light we'll see for a while. I thought we'd better stop now to take care of anything that needs taking care of." Hermod let out a deep breath as if that effort had been exhausting.

"Sounds good," Nick said.

Hermod handed Nick a waterskin then ducked down to the stream to fill some others. "Didn't have time to fill more than one before we left," he said.

Nick tilted his head back and squirted the water into his mouth. He was surprised at how thirsty he was. Riding with Hermod on Sleipnir at a bazillion miles an hour was obviously more work than he thought. For him anyway. Sleipnir, on the other hand, just stood there calmly, barely breathing hard, taking an occasional sip from the stream.

Sleipnir. Hermod. The cards, thought Nick. He remembered Baldur's card and the clues it had held, clues that might have saved his friend if he'd figured out Baldur's whole name in time. He tore into his pockets to see if there were cards for the two friends he was traveling with now.

Nick pulled out the deck and shuffled through until a blank card faced him. "Sleipnir," he said, and waited. The deck vibrated. A second later, an eight-legged horse appeared.

Clip-clip-clap, stamped Sleipnir, and tossed his head. Nick swore he was asking a question. "I have to say the name. Then the card appears." He held up the Sleipnir card. "This one's yours. It says:

> *Odin's eight-legged horse can pull any load. If you can recite your 8's table when this card is played to the field, you can play one card of your choice from the Sacrifice Pile to the Field.*

Clip-clop-clip, Sleipnir stamped.

Hermod still crouched next to the stream, filling another water skin. "That's true," he nodded. "I once saw Odin hook him up to a cart filled with all of the gold in a chamber . . . well, it was a big load," he finished, catching himself. "Do I have one?"

"Let's see," said Nick. He shuffled to another blank card. "Hermod," he said, and waited.

Nothing.

"Hermod," he said again. Still nothing.

Nick remembered what had happened with Baldur's card. "Hermod the Fast," he said.

Nothing.

"Hermod the Quick," he tried.

Still nothing.

Hermod stoppered another skin and walked over to Nick. "So those are the cards, eh?" he said. "My father told me you had some magic cards and that you were brought here by a card and had more cards with runes he couldn't read which aggravated him more than a little I'll tell you and that they had pictures of people and I guess horses too because Sleipnir's not a person no offense . . ."

Sleipnir gave a five-hooved stomp at the same time Nick said "Hermod!"

"Sorry," he said again. "What are you doing?"

"I have to get your name exactly right or it won't work," explained Nick. "Do people call you anything else?"

"Hermod the Handsome?" he said with a smile.

Sleipnir snorted.

"Hermod the Exceptionally Good-Looking?" he suggested, turning his head to the right so Nick could see his profile.

Nick laughed. "No really, is there anything people call you? Like with Baldur, I had to say 'Baldur the Good'."

Hermod thought for a moment. "I am fast and quick but not many people call me that. My Father calls me slow and thick but I think he's joking, well mostly joking anyway because I don't always think things through like the time I stole my mother's thimble and she chased me around the castle but I kept dodging her and she never would have caught me except I wasn't thinking and I ran outside in my nightclothes in the middle of a blizzard so I nearly froze before she let me back in and she said only the cold could catch her nimble thimble thief which was funny because then I caught a cold . . ."

Hermod stopped as Sleipnir gave a shrill whistle. Nick had caught it too.

"Hermod the Nimble," Nick said.

The deck vibrated and a picture of his blond-braided new friend appeared. Beneath it he read:

This son of Odin tried to bring Baldur back from Hela in Nif-fleheim. Add 20 to his attacks against gods.

"Well look at that," said Hermod, staring. "It is magic."

It was magic but Nick didn't think that it helped him very much. It just told him something he already knew, like Sleipnir's card had. Then it hit him.

"Hermod," said Nick. "The card says you try to bring Baldur back from Niffleheim."

"Right," said Hermod agreeably.

"It says you try to bring Baldur back."

"That's what we're doing," said Hermod, nodding.

"It doesn't say you actually do it," Nick insisted. "It says you *tried*."

Hermod crouched back down next to the stream to fill his last water skin. "And that's exactly what we'll do"

"But what if we can't bring him back?"

"Then it won't be for lack of trying." Hermod gave a pleased humphf of satisfaction at his logic and dipped the water skin into the stream.

"How can you say that!" yelled Nick. "What if we can't get him out and he has to stay there! How can you just sit there filling water bottles and think that's okay!!"

Hermod jerked at Nick's outburst. Looking at Nick with surprise, Hermod set the water skin aside, walked over, and squatted down so he was at Nick's eye level. He stared at Nick for a moment, his blue eyes calm and kind. Nick felt a rush of heat to his face and his hands shook. When Hermod finally spoke, it was in a quiet voice. "What more can you do than try your best?"

"Try harder!" Nick said.

"No," Hermod replied, shaking his head. "I mean try until you're exhausted. Try until every muscle quits. Try 'till your very breath is gone, your vision fails, and your mind goes gray. I mean try until there is nothing left." He put a hand on Nick's shoulder. "That is what I mean by your best. And, I ask you again, what more can you do than try your best."

"Do more," Nick said, but weakly this time.

"If you can do more, then it wasn't your best. Finding that little extra strength, that little extra speed, that little extra courage that you didn't think you had and using it, every drop of it, for something good. That's doing your best."

Now Hermod studied Nick. "That's what we're going to do, Nick Snow. We're going try our best to bring Baldur back." He paused. "Can you do that?"

When Hermod put it that way, Nick didn't know if he could. But he nodded.

"Good. Then if there's a way to get Baldur back, we will. And if there isn't, we'll know it." Hermod smiled and squeezed Nick's shoulder. "Right, Sleipnir?"

Clip-clap, stamped Sleipnir, and nodded.

When Nick smiled back, Hermod shook his head as if waking up and walked back to the water skins. "We'll need all these skins," he said over his shoulder, "because we won't be able to stop for hours and its going to be dark too so we won't be able to see even if we wanted to stop but we won't want to because when it's that dark you can't see what else is out there besides the water and you're really better off just going so Sleipnir will take us all the way to Gyoll bridge without a break which is just fine for him because he can go and go and go without stopping . . ."

So, Nick realized, could Hermod. This time he just let Hermod rattle on as the talkative man finished filling the water skin. Nick half-listened as the shadows lengthened and the sun set on Midgard. As the darkness grew and Nick thought about what Hermod had said, Nick realized he'd never tried that hard at anything in his life, at least not like Hermod described it. He didn't know, deep down, if he could. But for Baldur, he knew he'd try.

His very best.

Chapter 11

"Nick," said Hermod, shaking him gently. "Nick, wake up. We're getting close."

Nick opened his eyes. He shut them and opened them again. He couldn't tell the difference. Everything was black. Only the rapid-fire sound of Sleipnir's hoofbeats and the wind against his face let him know they were still galloping.

"How can you tell?" asked Nick, squinting. He couldn't even see Sleipnir's mane two feet in front of his face.

"Simple math," said Hermod. Nick could hear the pride in the speedy Norseman's voice as he explained. "We know it takes nine days for a normal horse to reach the bridge and a horse can travel 68,000 strides a day so when we couldn't see anymore I started counting Sleipnir's strides but since he has eight legs he covers 136,000 strides a day and of course Sleipnir is at least twice as fast as a normal horse so he'd travel the distance in half the time and then I remembered that a normal horse can only gallop for one-third of a day while Sleipnir never needs to stop so you divide the days by three which would have been easy but then I lost count of the strides and started over again so to make up for it I just multiplied by . . ."

"Hermod," interrupted Nick. "You don't have any idea where we are, do you?"

"Sure I do," said Hermod. His voice sounded a little offended but Nick couldn't see to be sure. "See that glimmer up ahead?"

Nick stared into the darkness. He may have been imagining it but he thought he saw the faintest pinprick of yellow light in the distance. "I think so," he said.

"That's Gyoll, the golden bridge. We'll be there soon."

"So all that counting business?"

"More to pass the time than anything else."

Nick focused on the pinprick of light, still not entirely sure it was there. There had been no break in the darkness since they'd entered what Hermod had called the Dark Glens—no stars, no moon, and certainly no sun. If Nick understood Hermod's math (and he wasn't at all sure he did), they had been riding for a little more than a day, pounding through one dark, narrow valley after another on the way to Niffleheim. He rubbed his eyes, feeling surprised, and a little guilty, that he'd fallen asleep on his quest to rescue his friend.

Now Nick shouldn't have been surprised that he'd fallen asleep and you shouldn't be either. From the moment he'd arrived in Midgard, Nick had been flying headlong from one hazard to another, first running away from dangers (mostly of the slobbering, howling, man-eating type), and now galloping towards them (mostly of the spooky, dead, underworldly type). He'd eaten a huge feast and then climbed on a horse that was so big that its back was more like a wide chair or a warm, soft couch. Then he'd ridden into the dark to the beat of regular, eight-legged strides that had rocked him ever so slightly. I'm getting sleepy just writing it and I haven't even had a giant chasing me or a wolf howling at me (not today anyway). And of course, although it's easy to forget because he was so brave, Nick was only eleven years old. He'd had a big day. So Nick was being a little hard on himself when he wondered how he could have fallen asleep since I think you'll agree with me that he was really doing rather well on this unexpected adventure.

Once he woke up though and stared into the blackness, Nick decided that there definitely was a pinprick of light up ahead and that it was definitely getting bigger. He was glad this dark ride might finally be over. Not because Nick was scared of the dark mind you. Nick had never been scared of the dark. In fact, one of his favorite times of the day was in the dark of early morning before his mom or dad or little brother were awake and he had the house all to himself.

No, Nick was glad the ride was almost over because he was bored. At home in the dark, he had a computer to check or a game to play or music to listen to. In this darkness, there was nothing. Surprisingly, the most interesting thing was Hermod. Nick found that when you have nothing to look at except the darkness and nothing to entertain you except conversation, Hermod's non-stop stream of talk wasn't so bad. This was especially true once Nick realized Hermod didn't mind being interrupted. In fact, the Norseman kind of expected it. He'd just go on a tear, rambling from one topic to another, and when he came to one Nick liked, Nick jumped in and stopped him on it. It wound up being kind of fun and had helped pass the time until Nick fell asleep.

At the moment though, Hermod was uncharacteristically quiet as the light continued to grow. Slowly, the faint yellow speck became a golden glow and the golden glow became a shimmering gold light and the shimmering gold light became a golden glare that nearly blinded Nick after the long hours of darkness. Squinting as his eyes adjusted, Nick saw a shining bridge of gold bricks and stone spanning a dark canyon. The great arching bridge shone with its own light and rose up into the sky, wide enough to carry at least twenty riders across at a time.

They reined up at the foot of the bridge. Sleipnir snorted in anticipation, as if he knew Baldur lay on the other side, giving no sign that he'd just run for more than a day to get there.

"That's right, Sleipnir," said Hermod, patting his side. "Let's give them some real thunder." Sleipnir snorted again and reared, four legs pawing at the air. Nick lurched forward and grabbed Sleipnir's rich mane with both hands, clenching his fists (and jaw and stomach). Sleipnir screamed and sprang for the bridge.

Sleipnir's hooves pounded on the golden stone, the sound thundering into the dark canyon below. The echoes bounced back to the bottom of the bridge, amplifying the sound until the thunder of Sleipnir's hooves rolled from the bridge to the canyon and back to the bridge again. The only thing Nick ever heard which compared to that thunder was the crash of waves breaking on the pier near his home right before a storm. And later, whenever he heard those pounding ocean waves, he always thought of Sleipnir and Gyoll, the golden bridge.

They galloped over the crest of the bridge and down the other side. Sleipnir rushed across the golden stone for the far side of the canyon. They were almost there when Sleipnir abruptly reared (on his back four legs). Nick had been too scared to pull his hands out of Sleipnir's mane, so he was ready when the horse rose up. But he was not ready for the woman who stood in the middle of the bridge, barring their way.

Her face was pale and faded blond hair hung loose about her shoulders. She wore a dress with a white bodice and a golden brown skirt. Her features were thin and fine and she seemed almost delicate. But beneath her delicate features, it seemed to Nick that she had a core of hard, unyielding ice. She was beautiful but there was no warmth in her.

"You don't look dead," she said, her fine eyebrows arching in surprise.

"That's a happy coincidence," said Hermod. "We're not."

"I have watched this bridge for countless years but never have I heard it shaken so." She stepped forward and patted the side of Sleipnir's jaw with a smooth, pale hand. Sleipnir humpfed and let her. "Is this Sleipnir?" she asked.

"How many eight-legged horses do you guys have running around here?" whispered Nick to Hermod.

"About as many as we have Floridians," whispered Hermod in reply. "Now mind your manners." To the woman he said, "It is."

"Seven companies of the dead passed just before you," she said, shaking her head. "Marching together they did not shake the bridge so." Sleipnir bowed his head and huffed softly.

"Seven companies passed?" asked Hermod.

"So I said."

"How long ago?"

"What meaning does time have to the dead?" she asked.

"A fair point, Bridge Maiden," said Hermod. "But we simply wonder how far ahead those companies are."

"And was Baldur with them?" Nick blurted. He knew he should keep quiet but he couldn't help it. He had to know if they were getting close.

The Bridge Maiden turned to face Nick, her eyebrows arching even more. "A Sun Warrior. And young too. We have not seen one of your people for many an age, even as we measure them." Her eyes seemed to glaze slightly and she said, "You are far from the warmth of your land. You must travel farther still, through darkness and cold and sorrow, before you return." Nick shivered, both at her words and the distant look on her face.

The Bridge Maiden's eyes sharpened, as if she were returning, as she kept stroking Sleipnir's jaw. "I have seen Baldur, Sun Warrior. He was in the sixth company to pass. He looked well," she added with a strange look on her face. "Very well indeed."

"Where is he going?" Nick asked.

Hermod gave Nick a nudge in the ribs. The Bridge Maiden looked at him as if he were young child. "Where all go," said the Bridge Maiden. "To Hela's palace." She looked back over her shoulder. "He will get there before you." She gave Sleipnir another pat on the jaw. "Even with Sleipnir carrying you." Sleipnir gently huffed again.

"Our thanks, Bridge Maiden," said Hermod. "But we must reach him."

"Then look in Hela's hall for he will already be there."

"Thank you, Bridge Maiden."

"Of course, the way for you will be blocked."

Hermod seemed surprised at that last statement. "Why?" he said in the shortest sentence Nick had ever heard him utter.

"Because you're not dead. So the gates of Niffleheim will be shut to you. And your friend will be on the other side."

"Then we'd best be off to see if we can catch him." Hermod tugged slightly on Sleipnir's reins and the horse reluctantly raised his head from the woman's hand. "Will you let us pass, Bridge Maiden?"

"Oh, I let all cross into Niffleheim," the Bridge Maiden said with a smile. Her face almost warmed as she gave Sleipnir a last pat. "It's when they try to get out that we have words."

"I'm sure we will," said Hermod. "Now if you'll excuse us . . ."

"Of course," she said, stepping back.

"Alright, Sleipnir. She said you couldn't catch him. Let's see." Hermod leaned into Nick and slapped the reins. "Hhhaaaaggghhhhh!" he cried. Instantly, Sleipnir took off at a full gallop.

Nick thought they'd gone fast before. But now they flew through the darkness.

★ ★ ★

Hermod gave the gates a push. Then he pounded on them with his fists. The steel gates shook but they didn't move. They were locked.

Hermod walked back to where Nick sat on Sleipnir. "They're locked," he said, shaking his head. "She wasn't kidding."

"Did you think she was?" asked Nick.

"I was hoping," said Hermod, scratching at his blond beard. "Because I'm not sure how to get past them."

Nick leaned back to take another look. Before them was a black steel gate. Two doors of the dark metal stretched high into the air, at least sixty feet. They looked so strong and thick that Nick didn't think a tank could break them down.

"Can we go around?" asked Nick.

A wall of dark gray stone stretched as far as he could see in both directions and rose so high that it disappeared into the darkness. Hermod pointed. "Do you see the end?" he asked.

Nick squinted. "No," he said.

"That's because there isn't one. You could ride forever in that direction and it would never stop. It wouldn't even curve. You'd just keep going and going and going and going and going . . ."

"It would keep going. Got it, Hermod."

"Right."

The two stared at the gate. Sleipnir shook his mane. The gate just sat there, a great black shadow in the pale light. Sleipnir stamped restlessly. No ideas came. Clip-clop-clip-clip, went Sleipnir.

"Would you settle down?!" snapped Hermod, grabbing Sleipnir's bridle. "You've been antsy ever since the Bridge Maiden was buttering you up."

Sleipnir snorted and shook his mane again.

"Don't think we didn't notice," grinned Hermod. He raised his voice and batted his eyelashes, "'Oh, is this the great Sleipnir? I've never heard such thunder before! It's amazing! He's so big and strong!'" His voice dropped back down to normal. "Then you standing there and letting her pat your head. Some war horse you are! I've never seen anything like it."

Sleipnir bowed his head and snorted. In the dim light, Nick thought Sleipnir actually looked embarrassed. For a horse.

Suddenly, Nick realized he'd been able to see ever since they'd crossed to this side of the bridge. "How can we see?" asked Nick.

Hermod cocked his head. "Eh?"

"How do we have enough light to see? There's no sun or moon."

"Oh," said Hermod. "It's the Shard. Over there." He pointed about a quarter of the way up the sky to where a thin sliver of pale light shone faintly. It was white and cold and Nick now saw that it cast the faintest of shadows on the ground. "It's an icicle. It hangs from the lowest branch of the Great Tree, Ygdrasill."

"An icicle that shines?" asked Nick.

"It catches the last light of the sun each day and reflects it here. Watch, you'll see that it slowly fades until it's renewed the next day."

Nick shook his head. He was so far from home that there wasn't even a moon anymore. He chuckled. "The cow jumped over the Shard."

Hermod looked up, his head swiveling from side to side. "I don't see a cow."

Nick laughed. "No, no, it's a rhyme from home. 'The cow jumped over the moon,' it goes. Somehow 'the cow jumped over the Shard' doesn't sound quite the same."

Sleipnir started to stamp again, a rapid clip-clip-clip-clop-clip.

"Is that what you've been on about?" Hermod asked the horse.

Sleipnir nodded and brought four hooves down in one big CLOP!

"What?" asked Nick, lost.

"The cow jumped over the moon you say?" Hermod asked. His eyes lit up. And it wasn't from the light of the Shard.

Nick felt very uneasy. "Yyeeeeeess," he said slowly.

"Well of course she did," said Hermod. With eyes twinkling, he began to work on the cinch of Sleipnir's saddle. "I've never seen a jumping cow myself although my brother once saw a leaping deer but I suppose those are a lot more common since everyone knows deer leap but I don't know of anyone who's ever seen a jumping cow and certainly not one that leapt over the moon because really I can't imagine a cow running that fast though I've seen some bulls run at a swift clip I'll tell you like when I went into one of Frey's fields and his bull didn't much take to my being there so I had to run and that's when I figured out I was fast because if I hadn't been I'd have been Hermod the Horn in the Bu. . . ."

"Hermod," interrupted Nick. "What are you doing?"

Hermod gave the saddle cinch one last tug. "Tightening the saddle of course."

Nick didn't want to ask but felt he had to. "Why?"

Hermod grinned. "Seems like a smart thing to do before we leap over the gate," he said and swung up into the saddle behind Nick.

"Nonononononononono," Nick said before he realized it. Heights weren't his thing and jumping sixty feet in the air wasn't his thing and splattering on stones definitely wasn't his thing. "This is a bad idea, Hermod. A really bad idea."

But Hermod was already reining Sleipnir away from the gate. "We'll need a good start," he said. Sleipnir neighed his agreement and galloped away from the wall.

"No, Hermod listen," said Nick desperately. "Sleipnir's the fastest horse I've ever seen and Odin said he could haul any load but Odin never said he could leap over anything like that."

"Odin did leave that out," Hermod said agreeably. He pulled Sleipnir around and the three faced the high, impossibly high, unjumpably high, black gates.

"He'd have to be able to fly," Nick said weakly.

"Let's hope not," said Hermod. "Because I'm pretty sure he can't do that."

"But nothing can jump that high! What if we hit the gates?"

"Best not to think about that," Hermod replied. "Ready, Sleipnir?"

Sleipnir neighed and shook his mane.

"Then let's go get Baldur. Hie!" he yelled and slapped the reins.

Sleipnir took off, his great eight-legged strides sending them hurtling towards the wall. Nick felt his face tighten with the speed as he was forced back into Hermod. He dug his hands into Sleipnir's mane, squeezing the thick hairs until his fingers and forearms felt like they were going to pop. "Ohmanohmanohmanohmanohmanohmanohmanoh manohman . . ." he muttered louder and louder as the gates rushed closer and closer . . .

Then, when Nick didn't think they could go any faster, Sleipnir uncorked another burst of speed. And leapt.

The bottom dropped out of Nick's stomach as they flew toward the top of the gate. All three of them screamed, the trio of man, boy, and horse shrieking a three part harmony of strain, fear, and exhilaration. Nick thought they'd smash into the gates like a coyote into a canyon wall but they just kept rising and rising and rising. Then they slowed down until, just for a moment, they seemed to float right at the top of the gate, hovering there in mid-air. And wonderfully, miraculously, Sleipnir cleared the top by no more than a mane's hair.

Then they started down.

As terrifying as the jump up had been, it was nothing to falling down. Now all three screamed in pure, one hundred percent, complete terror. The ground rushed toward them and they screamed louder and Nick didn't see how they could survive and the ground just kept coming and they were falling faster and faster and geez now he sounded like Hermod but it was getting closer and closer and here it comes and. . . .

Sleipnir landed. Just as gently as if he were setting a baby on a blanket.

Nick heard laughter, crazy laughter, and it took him a second to realize that one of the voices was his. Hermod was pounding him on the shoulder saying they'd made it and he was slapping Sleipnir on the shoulder telling him he'd done it and the two of them were laughing like wild men.

They'd made it. They'd leapt into Niffleheim.

Chapter 12

They were still laughing when they saw the castle. That stopped them.

Deep blue towers rose from the darkness. In the pale light of the Shard, the towers glimmered like the dark ice of a frozen lake. Nick didn't see any stones or joints or bricks. Instead, it looked like the whole thing had been carved from one giant, blue iceberg. As he rode closer and closer to the dark castle, Nick felt all of the joy of their jump drain out of him as he realized just what they'd jumped into.

Niffleheim. The Norse underworld.

Nick hadn't known exactly what to expect but so far it seemed dark and icy and unpleasant. As Sleipnir clopped through a huge, horseshoe-shaped gate, Nick remembered who they'd come to see and wondered if it was going to get worse. "What's Hela like?" Nick asked.

Before Hermod could answer, Nick's pocket began to vibrate. "Hang on," he said, and pulled out the deck.

A Hela card had appeared. Below a picture of a thin woman in a white dress, it said:

> *The daughter of Loki rules ice-cold Niffleheim, the Norse underworld.*

"Wait a minute," said Nick. "She's Loki's daughter?! We're supposed to get Baldur back from Loki's daughter?!"

"Yep," replied Hermod.

"But Loki's the one who killed Baldur!"

"That could make things a bit harder," admitted Hermod.

Nick thought for a moment. "What's she like?" He finally asked again.

Hermod hrrumphed. "She's as cold as her castle. None too pleasant either though I guess being trapped down here in the roots of Ygdrasill would get on anyone's nerves after awhile although she does seem to take it a little far because you'd think she would be a little civil once in a while but it doesn't matter who comes down here she just doesn't care even if Odin himself were to come down . . ."

"Hermod," interrupted Nick.

Hermod looked down. "One thing at a time?" he asked.

"Please," nodded Nick.

Hermod took a deep breath, held it, then exhaled. "Okay. Hela is the daughter of Loki and Angerbode, a giantess. Her brothers are Fenris Wolf, who you've met, and the Midgard Serpent, who it's best if you don't."

Nick knew snakes (you can't live in Florida without running into the occasional snake) and they didn't bother him much. "Is he poisonous or something?" asked Nick.

"Not sure," said Hermod. "He's so big I don't think anyone has ever checked."

"How big?" asked Nick.

"He encircles the world."

"Oh come on," said Nick.

"It's true. Ask Sleipnir."

Sleipnir nodded and huffed.

"Really?" asked Nick, still not quite believing.

Sleipnir huffed again.

"Your card said the same thing," said Hermod

"True," Nick agreed reluctantly.

"Anyway," continued Hermod. "The gods ignored Loki's children when they were young but you can't ignore a giant wolf, a monstrous snake, and an ill-tempered, ice blue woman for long. Especially when they start to misbehave."

"Ice blue?" asked Nick.

"Actually she's only half blue but that's beside the point. Eventually the gods had to get them under control. Odin threw the Midgard Serpent into the sea, bound Fenris Wolf with the Gleipnir chain, and sent Hela to Niffleheim to rule the undeserving dead. When she got here, she built this castle, Elvidner."

"Half-blue?" asked Nick, still stuck on her color.

"Yes, the left half actually. Frightfully grim too. Never cracks a smile. Always scowling. Completely humorless. No fun at parties."

Nick stared at the picture on his card again. Sure enough, Hela was half-blue. He'd missed it in the dim light. It was even the left half too.

"That's who we have to convince to let Baldur go?" Nick said, shaking his head.

"Yep."

"How are we supposed to do that?"

"Don't know," said Hermod. "I was hoping you did since Frigga sent you with me and I have no clue."

Nick thought a moment. "What does Hela want?"

"Nothing that I know of," said Hermod. "Except maybe to get out of here and wreak havoc with her brothers and father."

"That doesn't seem like much of an option."

"No. It isn't."

They clopped along in silence for a minute as Sleipnir took them deeper into the castle Elvidner.

"This might be hard," Nick said.

"That's what I thought too," replied Hermod.

They found their way to Hela easily enough. Or Sleipnir did anyway. The eight-legged horse guided them through a maze of dark hallways and drafty passages until they finally rode into a great hall. There was no doubting whose it was either. Because she was sitting at the other end on a big blue throne.

And when Nick saw her, he no longer thought it was going to be hard to get Baldur back. He thought it would be impossible.

"Time to get down," Hermod whispered and dismounted. Nick barely noticed as Hermod grabbed him under the arms and pulled him off Sleipnir and he barely felt Hermod's hand on his shoulder as the Norseman guided him towards Hela's throne. He couldn't take his eyes off Hela. And unfortunately, it appeared that she couldn't take her eyes off him.

Nick forced one foot after the other over the dark blue marble floor. Columns rose high above him on either side, making him feel smaller than he normally did with these huge people. But the still menace of those monstrous pillars was nothing compared to the cold glare of the woman who sat the blue throne.

She had finely chiseled features which might have been beautiful if they weren't so cold. She had pale blond hair and wore a pale white dress. Her pale blue eyes were cold and intense. And half of her, the left half, was blue.

"Look to her right," Hermod whispered. "She goes crazy if she thinks you're staring at the blue side."

Right, Nick thought. That's like telling someone not to think of a dancing polar bear in a pink tutu twirling a striped umbrella. (See?) Still, Nick tried to keep his eyes focused on her right side.

Hela, on the other hand, had no problem focusing on him. As Nick reached the foot of the throne, her flinty eyes bored in on him and her grim mouth tightened even more.

She looked from him to Hermod, like she was choosing between two ants. When she finally spoke, it was like the dry crack of ice dropped in warm soda pop. "Hermod. Why have you come? It is not yet your time."

"Lady Hela," Hermod said and bowed so deeply he touched one knee to the floor. He grabbed Nick by the cloak and pulled, forcing him to bow too. "We come because it was not yet the time of another who now sits in your halls."

"'We'," said Hela. "So Odin didn't trust you to do his bidding alone, did he Hermod? He sent this Sun Warrior to watch over you." Hela turned her grim gaze from Hermod back to Nick. Nick clenched his hands inside his fur so they wouldn't shake. "Congratulations," she said to him coldly. "You are the first Sun Warrior to pass into my realm. Perhaps you will be the first to stay."

Nick stood there, paralyzed at the thought of spending eternity with this half-frozen popsicle. Hermod nudged him and Nick realized Hermod actually expected him to talk.

"Lady Hela," he said, copying Hermod's form. "That would be great. But Odin has sent me on an urgent errand that I have to finish first."

"Odin doesn't rule here," Hela said harshly. "What errand of his brings you to me?"

Hermod made no move to answer so Nick took a deep breath, swallowed, and continued. "His son, Baldur. He died before he should have and he's been brought here. We've been sent to bring him back. With your permission," he added quickly.

Hela barked a sharp, humorless laugh. "All think they fall before their time. That's no reason to return him. You'll have to do better than that, Sun Warrior."

"Frigga told me to tell you that she will pay any ransom for her son's return," offered Nick.

Hela scoffed. "Death cannot be bought. Or life."

Hermod gave it a try. "Lady Hela, Frigga does not mean to offend you . . ."

"She does," Hela said coldly.

". . . she just loves her son and wants to find out what can be done to return him to Valhalla . . ." Hermod continued.

"Nothing," Hela replied.

". . . where all mourn his passing, from the gods. . . ,"

"Who put me here,"

". . . to the men . . ."

"Who fear to join me."

". . . to the animals . . ."

"Who flee at my approach."

". . . to the very trees and grass. . . ."

"Which refuse to grow in my realm."

". . . All of these things weep at Baldur's passing and desperately want him to return to Valhalla." Hermod raised both hands, holding them out from his sides. "If only you will let him."

Hermod argued so passionately and tried so hard to convince Hela, that Nick thought the big warrior might cry right there. That should convince her, Nick thought, and checked the goddess's reaction.

There were no tears in Hela's eyes. Only a sudden, cold light.

"You wouldn't lie to me, would you Hermod?" she said quietly.

Nick could sense something was coming but he couldn't tell what it was. Hermod didn't seem worried as he charged straight ahead. "Of course not, Lady Hela."

Hela's lips curled in what was, almost, a frosty smile. "Fine. If what you say is true, then I will release Baldur."

Nick grabbed Hermod's arm in excitement, unable to believe they'd done it. Hermod smiled down at Nick, obviously relieved that Hela was letting Baldur go. He turned back to Hela. "Where is he? Or will we go back to Valhalla and find him there?"

Hela raised an eyebrow (the blue one). "Who?"

"Baldur," said Hermod. "Where do we find Baldur so we can take him back."

"You're not taking him back," said Hela with the slightest look of satisfaction on her face.

"What do you mean!?" yelled Nick. "You said you'd let him go!"

"The last person to speak to me like that found himself trapped for eternity in a pitch black iceberg." Nick realized he'd yelled and quickly bowed his head. "That's better," Hela said coldly. "I said, Sun Warrior, that I would release him if what Hermod says is true. You have told me that every living thing mourns Baldur. If that's true, I will release him."

Hermod just stared as he realized what he had said. "They do," he said weakly.

"That's not good enough, Hermod," said Hela. She leaned forward on her throne, her pale hair swinging forward alongside her half-blue face. "You tell Odin and Frigga that Baldur can return if every living thing weeps for him. Every god, every hero, every monster, every animal, every tree, every blade of grass in Asgard and Midgard.

Every single one must shed a tear for Baldur. If they do, he is free to leave. If even one does not, he stays with me." Hela sat back on her throne, crossing her pale arm over her blue one. "Forever."

Nick stared at her, his mouth half-open. He was far too mad to care how dangerous his look must have been. Hela had pretended to let Baldur go, got them to believe he was coming home with them, and then set a task so impossible it would never happen. It was one of the cruelest things anyone had ever done to him (and don't forget a giant had tried to eat him a few days ago).

Hermod didn't seem to mind though. "Okay," was all he said as he put a hand on Nick's arm. "We'll tell Odin and Frigga. How long do we have?"

"I want to hear the world sobbing by the end of a fortnight."

"Fourteen days then," Hermod nodded. "Fine."

Nick didn't know how Hermod could stay so calm. He was sure they would never see Baldur again. As if Hermod read his mind, he asked, "Can we see him?"

"I wouldn't want Frigga to think I'd misplaced her pup," Hela said with a dismissive wave. "You can talk to him. For one hour. Then you will go. He's feasting in the west hall."

"Thank you, Lady Hela," replied Hermod. "C'mon," he whispered under his breath. "Thank her and let's go."

"But she didn't do anything," whispered Nick.

"She did more than we could have expected," hissed Hermod. "Now do it!"

"Thank you, Lady Hela," Nick said. He bowed and turned to leave.

"What do your cards say about me, Sun Warrior?" called Hela after him.

Nick froze. How could she know about the cards? Nick didn't know what to think but he knew this wasn't good. His back still to her, he answered, "What cards?"

"The cards you carry," her dry voice cracked. "The cards that brought you here. The cards my father wants."

Nick slowly turned to face her. "What do they say about me?" Hela repeated.

She knew he had the cards so he couldn't deny it. But Nick found he didn't want to talk about them. Or show them to her.

"They say 'Lady Hela is the fair goddess who rules Niffleheim from her majestic castle. Her beauty is surpassed only by her generosity.'"

She barked another laugh like cracking ice. "You lie," she said. She stared at him for another moment. "But I wouldn't tell me either."

She waved a hand. "Go. Baldur waits for you. But if you stay more than an hour, you stay forever." Then Hela smiled, a horrible, gleaming, evil smile that gave Nick nightmares long after he left Niffleheim. "And I will have my first Sun Warrior."

"Move it," whispered Hermod. "Before she changes her mind."

The two hurried across the gleaming blue hall back to where Sleipnir waited for them. Then they mounted and headed for Baldur as fast as Sleipnir could gallop.

A cold blue light filled the dark blue hall. Row after row of sturdy wooden tables stretched into the distance. Thousands of men and women sat on benches, eating. Except for the clatter of plates and knives, the hall was silent. Not one person spoke.

Nick and Hermod again left Sleipnir in the passageway and entered. Nick couldn't tell where the pale blue light came from but it seemed to follow them, weakly illuminating everything they passed. Nick went straight to the head of the table were a man with a red beard and braids was methodically tearing apart a chicken. A light silver armring with a red ruby glimmered faintly on his left arm. The man was wiping chicken grease from his fingers when he saw Nick.

"No!" the man cried and sprang to his feet. "You can't be here! Lad, what happened? How did they kill you?!"

"Baldur!" cried Nick and rushed toward his first Norse friend, not really hearing what Baldur had said. Nick stretched his arms out to hug Baldur when he skidded to a stop. "Wait. Are you . . .?"

"A spirit? A wraith? A ghost?" Baldur asked with a twinkle. Nick nodded.

"No, lad. This is where I belong. So I'm solid as a tree trunk. See?" He thumped his chest once with a fist. Baldur's blue eyes remained intensely focused on Nick and his eyebrows stayed scrunched together in a mixture of anger and concern. "But you," he continued. "Why are you here? How did you die? And Hermod, you too?" he said, looking over Nick's head. "How could that have happened?"

Nick suddenly understood his friend's fear. "We're not dead! We came looking for you!"

Baldur's eyes lightened with obvious relief. "Odin's Crows that's good news!" He put one arm around Nick's shoulders to hug him and reached out with the other to clasp Hermod's arm. "I was afraid someone had killed you too. Both of you." Then his grin faded and it was Baldur's turn to look puzzled. "What do you mean you were looking for me?" he asked Nick.

Nick looked at Hermod then back to Baldur. "It's kind of a long story," said Nick. "And we don't have much time."

"Then we know who shouldn't tell it," said Baldur with a smile at Hermod.

"Hey!" said Hermod, laughing. "That's not fair. Once I told a story to Odin when he was in a hurry and didn't think he had time to listen to it but I went ahead anyway and spoke so fast that. . . ." Hermod stopped and smiled, looking a little embarrassed. "Maybe Nick should tell the story."

Baldur and Nick shared a smile. "Good idea," said Baldur, clearing a place at the table. "Sit," he said with a wave. "And speak quickly."

Nick rattled off their tale as fast as he could—he described Baldur's murder and Odin's attempt to keep Baldur's spirit in

Valhalla. He told of Frigga's grief and her irresistible request that Nick bring Baldur back. He recounted the long journey he and Hermod and Sleipnir had made and finished by telling Baldur about Hela's hopeless deal for his return.

Baldur listened to it all intently. He shook his head and muttered when Nick identified Loki as the one who gave Hador the mistletoe. He became very still when Nick described Frigga's tears. He laughed and slammed the table with one hand when he heard about Sleipnir's leap. And surprisingly, Baldur did not seem the least bit distressed by Hela's impossible bargain.

"How can you be so calm about it?" Nick asked when he finished. "We'll never be able to make the whole world cry!"

Baldur smiled and shrugged. "It's more of a chance than I had yesterday."

The pressure to bring Baldur back made Nick feel like he was wearing a backpack full of bricks. "But what if we fail?" His voice cracked at the thought.

"Then that was the fate woven for me and I'll stay here." He picked up a leg of chicken and took a big, greasy bite. "See? Tasty."

Hermod grabbed a leg for himself and tore off a chunk. "Ishhold."

"What?" said Nick and Baldur.

Hermod swallowed and grimaced. "It's cold."

Baldur waved a hand down the table and shrugged again. "It all is. We are in Niffleheim you know."

For the first time, Nick noticed, really noticed, the other people at the endless table. The men and women, many old, lining the table kept eating their food silently and methodically. No steam rose from the plates, although Nick thought he saw a hint of it from their breath. No one seemed miserable or anguished or sad but they certainly didn't seem happy either. Resigned might be a word his dad would use to describe it. It reminded Nick of a lunch period where everyone's mom had packed them something they didn't really like but that they had to eat anyway; food that was perfectly acceptable and probably nutritious but wasn't warm, wasn't tasty, and wasn't good.

Nick couldn't help but compare it to the delicious, lively feast they'd shared in Valhalla. The thought that Baldur would have to stay here if he failed added another brick to Nick's backpack.

It must have shown on Nick's face because Baldur put a hand on his shoulder and said, "Don't worry about me, lad. This is the highest level of Niffleheim and they really treat me quite well. Though she'd never admit it, Hela knows my father put her here and I think she believes he could still make things worse for her if he were upset."

Nick couldn't tell whether to believe him but gave Baldur a smile anyway. It's what his Norse friends seemed to do. The bigger the danger, the worse the situation, the bigger they smiled and the less they seemed to care.

"Besides, there are some advantages to passing on to the underworld," Baldur continued.

"All you can eat chicken?" asked Hermod with a slight smile.

"Free ice?" Nick chimed in, following Hermod's example.

"Knowledge," said Baldur.

"Of what?" asked Nick.

"Of you, lad."

Nick cocked his head in an unspoken question.

"I know now why Loki killed me," Baldur said. He put a hand on Nick's shoulder. "I think he's after you too."

Nick's stomach turned and he thought he might throw up. Baldur's hand steadied him and he could feel Baldur and Hermod watching him. Though he felt sick and scared, he'd had enough of both. He decided to be Norse.

Nick raised his head and grinned. "Great. Does he want to eat me too? Tell him to get in line."

"I doubt you're to his taste, lad." Baldur squeezed Nick's shoulder. "Though maybe with a little salt and pepper . . . What do you think, Sleipnir?" Baldur called.

Clip-clip, Sleipnir stamped in agreement from the corridor.

Baldur chuckled. "I always liked that horse." He returned his attention to Nick. "There's nothing to worry about though, lad," he said.

"Of course not," replied Nick, shaking his head. "The god of mischief just wants to kill me. Why would I worry?"

"No truly, lad. You don't have to worry."

Nick cocked his head. Baldur smiled.

"Because I know how to keep you alive until you can get home."

Chapter 13

"How?" Nick asked. "How can you protect me if you couldn't . . . I mean if he could kill . . ." Nick trailed off, wanting to know the answer but not wanting to offend Baldur.

"How can I protect you if I couldn't protect myself?" said Baldur, still smiling. Nick nodded, relieved he didn't have to say it. "An excellent question, lad, and one I'd want to know the answer to if I were standing in your boots. It'll take a little bit to explain though."

"That's no problem," said Hermod. "Sometimes you need a longer story to understand what's happening like when I had to tell Thor how I had accidentally worn his gauntlets of strength and wound up throwing a cow across . . . Oh, right," stopped Hermod as he noticed Baldur's glare. "Shutting up."

Baldur looked up for a moment and crossed his arms, putting one hand on his silver armring. He absently rubbed the red stone in its center as he gathered his thoughts.

Finally, he looked back down and said, "You know my mother made everything promise not to hurt me?"

"Sure," nodded Nick. "Except mistletoe."

"Except the mistletoe," agreed Baldur. "Do you remember why she did it?"

"Because she was scared something would happen to you."

"Right. She dreamt I died and was so upset, she traveled the entire world and made every single thing promise not to harm me."

Nick nodded again, a little impatient. He knew all this. Baldur had told him about it the first time they'd met.

"My mother loves me very much. But that's only part of the story. I didn't know the rest until after I died."

"The rest?" asked Hermod, raising his blond eyebrows.

"The other reason she made everything promise," continued Baldur. "The other reason she made it almost impossible to hurt me."

"She was creating a Talisman."

Nick cocked his head to the side in question. "A talis-what?"

"A Talisman. A thing with special power. A powerful magic."

Nick must have looked as confused as he felt because Baldur hurried on. "Think about what it means to go to everything in the world. People and animals and rocks and trees and water. *Everything.*"

"That does seem like a lot."

"Now, think about what she had to do. She couldn't just tell everything 'don't hurt my son.' She has lots of sons."

Hermod nodded.

"And think how hard it would be to describe me to, oh, a badger or an elderberry bush or a horse."

There was a snort and loud CLOP! from the hallway.

"Sorry," called Baldur to Sleipnir. "Most horses," he corrected. "Those things can't tell the difference between one man and another. They wouldn't have been able to recognize me."

Nick nodded. If he hadn't seen the promise work, he might not have believed all this. But he had, so he did.

"So she gave them all a way to know it was me." Baldur slid the silver armring off his arm. The cold light of the hall reflected palely off the red stone in the center as he held it up. "This."

Nick stared more closely at the braided silver-white metal band and the two snarling wolves holding a ruby in their mouths. "Your armring?" he asked.

"My armring," nodded Baldur. "This is how they recognize me and know not to hurt me."

Nick didn't want to be rude but he couldn't take it anymore. "Baldur, so what?! How does Frigga's promise for you keep someone from killing me?!" he snapped. Nick regretted his outburst immediately and lowered his head. "Sorry," he said.

"Don't be sorry, lad," grinned Baldur. "It's a good question." He slapped Nick's shoulder. "And you asked it like a Norseman too."

Baldur leaned forward, still grinning. "I'll tell you how Frigga's promise helps you. Frigga didn't make everything promise not to hurt me. She made everything promise not to hurt whoever wore the armring." His blue eyes sparkled as he held out the silver and ruby armring.

"And I'm giving it to you."

Nick didn't take it. He just stared at the silver circle, not sure he was following what Baldur had said. "So all those things didn't promise not to hurt you?" he said.

"No," Baldur said. "They promised not to hurt the person wearing the armring. Think about it. Think about what she made you promise."

Nick remembered Frigga accusing him of wanting to hurt Baldur and how she had made Nick swear not to hurt him. Recalling what Frigga had made him say, Nick murmured, "I give my oath that I will not harm the man who stands before me wearing the silver and ruby armring . . ." Nick's eyes widened as he heard himself say the words. He thought he'd sworn not to harm Baldur. But he hadn't.

"Why does everyone tell the other story then?" asked Nick.

"They don't know the truth," said Baldur. "I don't think Odin even realizes it." Baldur shook his head. "Frigga didn't tell me how it worked either. She just gave me the armring for a present and told me she'd be very upset if I didn't wear it."

Nick nodded, remembering a watch from his mother he'd worn for a year for the same reason. "So why would Frigga make all this up?"

"That part's easy. What would happen if people knew I had an armring that made me invulnerable?"

"Everyone would try to take it," Nick guessed right away (I told you he was smart).

"Exactly," nodded Baldur. "Especially . . ."

"The giants," interrupted Hermod excitedly. "The giants would try to take it from you because they know we'll fight at Ragnarok and if they learned you had something that could make them invulnerable they'd be on you like white on snow, like fur on a bear, like a three-legged otter on . . ."

"Hermod," said Baldur and Nick together.

"Right. Got it," Hermod said and clamped his beard together.

"He's right," said Baldur. "Especially the giants. They'd want it for themselves."

Nick was still working through what Baldur was telling him. "So all this time, nobody figured out that anyone could wear the armring?"

Baldur shook his head. "Frigga was very careful in the way she worded her oath and the story of her dream reinforced the belief that the promise was just for me. The more people heard the story, the less they thought about the armring until eventually everyone just assumed I was the one who was invulnerable."

"When it was the armring all along," said Nick. A sudden thought hit Nick. "So Frigga wanting you back, in Valhalla. Does she love you, or does she just want . . ." he trailed off, not wanting to say it.

Baldur's eyes softened at Nick's concern. "She loves me, lad. More than anything. She also needs to get the Talisman back."

"But she was so upset," Nick said. "When she sent us to find you, she was crying. I thought she just wanted you back with her in Valhalla."

"She does, lad. There's no reason her love and her responsibility can't work together."

Even though he knew it was true, it still seemed different to Nick. He had been sure Frigga's grief at Baldur's loss had been real but now he couldn't help thinking that there had been more to it, that she had also wanted something from him. Something very important.

Baldur stared at Nick, seemingly reading his mind. "She wants me back, lad, and she'll do anything to accomplish it. If anyone can make everything in the world weep, it's her."

"I hope so," Hermod muttered quietly.

"But," Baldur continued, ignoring his brother. "That might not happen. And if I don't return, it will do more than break my mother's heart. It will leave the gods without a weapon they need. And that's the other reason you have to take it, lad." Baldur held out the armring again. "You've got to get it out of here so that my father has it at Ragnarok."

Nick still didn't take it. "Why me? Why not give it to Hermod?"

"Because Loki is trying to get you."

Nick's spine went cold again. He'd almost forgotten that part. "But why would Loki want to hurt me? I haven't done anything to him."

"There's no telling with Loki." Baldur spat the name, his scowl fierce (you'd be a tad irritated with someone who killed you too). He shook his head. "He's plotting something. At the very least, he learned that Frigga missed the mistletoe. But he may have figured out the part about the armring too." Baldur shook his head. "And he spends far too much time with giants."

Hermod grunted in agreement but kept his mouth clamped shut.

A flash hit Nick. "The cards. He wants the cards too."

Baldur and Hermod turned to Nick.

"How do you know that?" asked Baldur.

"Hela. I didn't catch it at the time but she said it. She said her father wants my cards." Nick unconsciously put his hand under his furs and felt the outline of his deck. "But why?"

Baldur scratched his red beard for a moment. "Take out your cards."

Nick reached into the pocket of his black furs and pulled out his Norse deck. Their blue backs shimmered like ice in the pale blue light. He showed Baldur the new cards that had appeared since he died, including his own. "I don't look like that," Baldur said.

"You kind of do," said Hermod.

"Hmmphf," grunted Baldur. They leafed through all the pictured cards until they came to the blank cards. There were still quite few. "Maybe the answer is there," he said. "Maybe Loki wants the deck because of a card that hasn't appeared yet." Baldur thought a little longer. "Show me your card."

Nick leafed through the blue cards until he came to the lone red one. "That card is different," said Baldur. "I still can't read it but it's not like the other ones."

"Well, yeah. It's red."

"Not the color. The card itself." Nick pulled the red Adventure card out of the deck of blue Norse cards. And there it was. *Nick Snow had never seen it. That was about to change.* It sure had. He'd gone from never seeing it to never wanting to see it again. And then, *The Adventure Card is the Key. Brace yourself.*

"That card is the key," said Baldur.

"I thought you couldn't read it," said Nick.

"I can't," said Baldur. "I'm telling you the card is the key to how you got here. It's not a normal part of that deck. It was added."

"By who?"

"By whoever wanted to bring you here." Baldur shook his head. "I don't know who did it, or even why. But I know someone added this card to the deck and linked it to you so that it would bring you to Midgard."

"How do you know that?" asked Nick.

"It's tough to keep secrets from the dead," Baldur replied. "When I died, I learned things. Not everything, but enough to figure out how you got here."

"Did you learn how to get me back?" Nick asked hopefully.

Baldur's face fell a little. "No, lad. I'm sorry. But that card is the key to it."

Nick tried to hide his disappointment but it must not have worked. Baldur put a hand on his shoulder and said, "Don't worry, Odin will figure it out. We just have to keep you out of Loki's hands until then." He held the armring out one more time. "Take the armring."

Much as he wanted its protection, one last thing held Nick back. "But I don't want to stay until the end of time and fight the giants," he said.

Baldur laughed, his eyes twinkling. "Is that what this is about? You don't have to fight, lad. Just wear it while you are on your quest, until you find your way home, to keep you safe. Then before you leave, give it to the most worthy warrior you find. Let him do the fighting." Baldur gave one last chuckle before his eyes took that same calm, relentless look they'd had at the rainbow bridge. "It's yours, lad. Take it."

Nick reached out and took the armring. The metal was smooth and slightly warm though everything around them was cold. "Wait a minute," said Nick. "How is this here? Shouldn't it be back . . . well, you know . . ."

"On my body?" asked Baldur. Nick nodded. "The talisman is linked to the spirit of its owner. When I came here, it followed me. Now though, it belongs to you. Put it on."

Nick slid the ring onto his arm, twisting it around so the wolves' heads and the ruby faced out. He waited for a tingling or a buzz or a glow. "I don't feel anything," he said.

"You won't," said Baldur. Quick as a blink, Baldur grabbed a cup and whipped it at Nick's head. They were so close,

Nick didn't have time to duck as the cup zipped straight for him. Right before the cup smacked him between the eyes, it turned aside and clattered to the floor. The sound echoed across the silent hall. "But it still works," Baldur said with a smile.

Baldur reached over and pulled Nick's fur cloak tightly around him, covering Nick's arms. "Keep it hidden," he said. "If Loki doesn't know you have it, he won't think to use mistletoe against you. Instead, he'll just use things that it can protect you from."

Nick nodded.

"And don't tell anyone about it. Not even Frigga. Otherwise Loki will find out."

Nick nodded again.

"That means you keep your mouth shut!" Baldur said, pointing at Hermod.

Hermod made a motion of locking a key in his mouth and throwing it away.

The pale blue light around them dimmed and the hall seemed to grow colder. Nick barely noticed but it seemed important to Baldur; he looked over his shoulder and talked more quickly.

"And remember, the armring must be given to someone to get its protection. They can't take it from you. So don't let anyone trick you into giving it away before you must." Nick nodded.

"Good," said Baldur with a quick breath. "That's all I can do to help you, lad. You'll have to do the rest on your own."

There was a CLOP! and a snort from the hall. "With the help of your friends." There was a clip-clip-clap-clip of agreement.

The temperature in the hall fell further and their breath began to steam. "Ride back to Valhalla," Baldur continued. "Tell Frigga and Odin of Hela's bargain. Guard the armring and find a worthy warrior for it. And above all keep it out of Loki's hands."

The full weight of what Baldur wanted him to do pressed on Nick's shoulders, making him slump. "But I'm only a kid. How can I take on Loki?"

Baldur's eyes became stern and his hand gently, but irresistibly, lifted Nick's chin. "You are Nick Snow, Sun Warrior and Floridian, Wolf Passer and Steed Rider, Crosser of the Rainbow, Leaper of the Gates, Holder of the Cards, Traveler of the Great Tree from the highest leaves of Asgard to the deepest roots of Niffleheim." With a quiet intensity, he leaned forward and said each word distinctly. "If someone must stand against Loki, I can think of none better."

"I don't want to leave you here," Nick said. He felt tears well from the bottom of his eyes.

Baldur let go of Nick's chin and put a hand on his shoulder. The gentle smile returned. "You can only free me if you go."

"That's not fair."

"But it's true. And truth, no matter how painful, is all a warrior cares about."

Nick grabbed the massive hand on his shoulder and squeezed for all he was worth. "I'll bring you back."

"I know. So go do it."

The cold was seeping up from the floor through Nick's thick fur boots and the steam of his breath had become thick as smoke. "If you stay past the time Hela has given you, you must stay forever," said Baldur. "You have to leave. Now."

Nick felt a prickling burn as his tears froze in his eyes. He couldn't stand the thought of leaving Baldur again and stepped forward, arms out, to hug him. Baldur raised a hand, stopping Nick.

"The time for tears is done," he said and he scowled pointedly at Nick's outstretched arms. "Go. Free me. And guard the Talisman." Then Baldur turned and walked away.

Nick stopped, his arms still hanging out there, startled by Baldur's abrupt exit. He stared at his friend's massive back as Baldur strode away down the long, silent table. Seeing Baldur again was making the pain of losing him worse. But more than that, Nick felt hurt by Baldur's coldness when he left.

"Baldur," Nick yelled, unsure what he'd done. "What if I don't know what to do? What if I mess it up?!"

Baldur stopped. He kept his back to Nick for a moment. Then he straightened and turned. Though he smiled, a thin line of ice trailed from the corner of each eye. "You can do it, lad," said Baldur quietly. "A man who can walk past a wolf can do anything." Then he quickly turned and strode away.

"Come on, Nick," said Hermod. Nick saw that the swift Norseman's beard was coated with ice. "I think we're about

out of time. And I don't know about you but I like my chicken hot off the spit."

Nick turned toward the entrance and found that his boots stuck slightly to the floor. He looked down to find that a thin coat of ice surrounded the black fur of his boots and spilled over onto the floor. Much longer, and it would have been difficult to move. He pulled each boot free with a snap and started toward the door.

"Hot and spicy chicken for me," he said as Hermod walked beside him. "Although not as spicy as my dad likes. He gets buffalo wings so hot his head sweats."

"Buffalo?" said Hermod as they walked toward Sleipnir. "What kind of chicken is that?"

"It's not a chicken. It's like a cow only with a big hairy head and shorter horns."

Hermod shook his head. "Yours is a strange land, Nick Snow. The sun is so bright that your skin is dark and the air is so warm that your cows fly."

"Cows fly?" said Nick. "What are you. . . . No, no, no. Buffalo wings are chicken wings. They're chicken wings dipped in a spicy sauce."

Hermod scowled. "You call your chickens buffalos?"

"No, no. Only their wings."

Nick and Hermod stopped in front of Sleipnir, who was stamping all eight of his legs to keep warm. Hermod shook his head again. "I don't think I'd like your land. Things sound strange there."

The Norseman reached under Nick's armpits, set him on Sleipnir, and swung up behind him. Then the eight-legged horse carried Nick down the icy blue corridor of Hela's underworld castle as he set out on a new quest to save his dead friend by making everything in the world weep.

Nick shook his head and laughed. "I know what you mean."

Chapter 14

"She wants what?!" Odin roared. "I'll give her weeping. And it'll start with her!"

The blast of Odin's voice knocked Nick back into Hermod's chest. Hugin and Munin squawked and flapped their great black wings, their talons lifting off Odin's shoulders as their wings whirred through the air. They settled back down after a moment. Odin didn't.

"And you just left him there?!" His one eye blazed. "How could you find him and leave him there?!"

"Odin!" snapped Frigga. Her voice stopped the All-Father in mid-rant. "You know very well that they couldn't have brought Baldur back against Hela's will. *You* can't even do that! That's why we sent Nick and Hermod in the first place." She patted Odin's hand. "They couldn't very well break Baldur out if they were frozen to the Hall floor."

Odin and the crows sat, quietly considering Frigga's scolding. Then the crows began to whisper in Odin's ears. Even though Nick had been to the underworld, the crow whispering still gave him the willies. When Odin finally spoke, it was much quieter and, thankfully, calmer.

"Then what will we do?" asked Odin.

"What Hela says," said Frigga calmly. The crows whispered faster.

"Make everything in the world weep? Are you crazy?"

The glow in Frigga's eyes was no less bright than Odin's. "Have you forgotten what I did before? I made every living thing but one promise not to hurt Baldur. I can make them weep that I failed."

Odin shook his head. "And have you forgotten how long it took you? How exhausted you were by the time you finished?"

"So we'll be tired. So what. We'll have Baldur back. It's a small price to pay."

"But she wants it done in fourteen days," said Odin. "How will we do that?"

Frigga waved a hand. "Last time I checked, you have a hall full of heroes doing nothing but eating and drinking. Send them."

"But they have to prepare for . . ."

"Ragnarok, I know," said Frigga sharply. "But I haven't heard Heimdall's horn today have you?" Odin wisely remained silent. "I don't think the battle at the end of time is going to happen this afternoon. Your heroes can take two weeks off."

"But they can't stop training . . ."

"They'll be criss-crossing the world. Call it cross-training."

The Ruler of the Gods actually looked flustered as he stared at his wife. His lips moved twice but no sound came out.

Frigga put a hand on Odin's arm. "Send them, husband. Send them with a message to every living thing." The crows stopped whispering as her voice dropped. "Tell them to weep for your son."

Odin's beard was bristly as a white broom. Then his jaw and his beard relaxed and he nodded his head, once. "I'll tell them," he said softly. Putting one great arm around her shoulder, he bent down (crows and all), kissed Frigga on the forehead, and strode out of the hall to assemble his heroes.

Nick and Hermod started to leave. Frigga turned from Odin to them. "Hermod," she said with unusual sharpness. "Put that speed of yours to some use and go help my husband. Sun-Warrior," she looked at Nick. "Stay here."

Hermod bowed, giving Nick a quick look and a shrug that said "I don't know" and left. Frigga said nothing. The two stared at each other without speaking as Hermod's boots slapped softly on the stone floor. It wasn't until the echo of those steps died completely that Frigga spoke.

"So what did my son tell you?" she asked.

"He told me that you didn't protect him because you loved him," Nick replied coldly. "He said you protected him for other reasons."

Frigga winced and widened her eyes at the same time, which is not easy. (Try it.) "He said that?"

"Not exactly," admitted Nick. "But after he told me about the armring, it wasn't hard to see."

Frigga's face showed her surprise. Nick kept going and, before he knew it, all his suspicions about Frigga's motives poured out. "You talked me into going to Niffleheim because you told me you loved him. I agreed to go because I did too." Nick shook his head. "But you didn't care about Baldur. You really just wanted the armring back."

Frigga's stare would have made Hugin and Munin fly away. Because he had no wings, Nick stood there and took it. "You don't know what you're talking about," said Frigga, her voice now cold.

"Yes, I do. You gave me all that garbage about wanting to save Baldur but you just wanted him to bring the armring back." An idea hit Nick. "And that's the reason you made everything promise not to hurt him in the first place—to create the Talisman." The thought made everything boil up inside of Nick—his anger at being here, his anger at being chased all the time, and worst of all, his anger at leaving Baldur behind. "You told everyone that you loved Baldur and that you had a bad dream that something terrible was going to happen to him but it was all a lie. You just spread the story of the promise and the dream and your love to hide what you were really doing—making a weapon to use against the giants. You don't care about Baldur at all."

Nick didn't even realize he was shouting at the goddess until he stopped. Angry and unrepentant, he stood there, fists clenched, and waited for a bolt of lightning to strike him. Or to be turned into a toad.

Frigga didn't vaporize him or even shout back. She just shook her head. "You're wrong, Sun Warrior," she said quietly. "It's true I made the armring into a talisman we could use against the giants. I knew that whoever I picked to wear the armring would be invulnerable." She shook her head. "But I couldn't bear the thought of something happening to Baldur. So I gave it to him. I gave Baldur the armring *because* I loved him, because I didn't want anything to hurt him, because the armring would make *him* invulnerable."

Despite everything he had thought, Nick could feel Frigga's love for Baldur as she explained what she'd done. It made him feel a little ashamed of himself.

"I wanted to protect him from everything," continued Frigga. She smiled sadly and shook her head. "Almost everything. For the magic to work, I had to pick one thing the armring would not protect against. Just one thing. So I picked a small, rare little bush, a harmless plant that could never hurt him. The mistletoe. Then I kept it a secret."

"But Loki found out," said Nick.

"Loki found out," agreed Frigga. "He probably wanted the armring for himself and figured he could get it once Baldur was dead. He wouldn't have known that it follows the owner's spirit until it is given to someone else. But since Baldur didn't give it to anyone before he. . . ."

Frigga stopped. She studied Nick, her green eyes suddenly hard. Her intense stare made Nick so self-conscious that he felt like his fly was open.

"What else did he tell you?" she asked.

"Nothing," Nick said. "That's it."

"You talked about the armring." There was no question in the statement.

"Yes."

Frigga leaned forward. "Did he give it to anyone?"

Nick was a very truthful boy. Only Baldur's stern warning kept him from blabbing. He didn't want to lie to Frigga. But he did.

"No," he replied.

"Truly?"

"Truly."

Frigga bowed her head. "Then no one will be able to take it from him." Her head seemed to grow heavier as she rested it on her hand. "Our last hope at Ragnarok is gone. Without an invulnerable hero, we cannot hope to stand against the giants at the last battle."

"Unless we get him back," said Nick.

Frigga looked up. "If we get him back, he can use it," Nick continued. "Or give it to someone who can."

"Of course," Frigga said wearily. "We only have to make the whole world weep. In fourteen days."

The raw fatigue and grief on Frigga's face convinced Nick that the goddess was missing more than her son's armring— she missed her son and feared for her people. He flexed his arm, feeling the tightness of the armring. He wanted to tell her that they had been partially successful, that they had re- trieved the talisman the gods needed to face the giants, that there was hope. But Baldur's directions not to tell anyone had been clear and Nick knew he had to follow them. Still, he wanted to say something, anything, to make her feel bet- ter. "We can do it," he said finally. "You did it before. And you have help this time."

Frigga looked at Nick for a moment, then smiled faintly. "Yes," she said. "Yes I do." She stood and held out a hand. "We'd better get started."

Hand in hand, the majestic goddess and the young sun warrior left Odin's hall and set out on their mission to make the world cry.

Nick hoped they had a lot of onions.

You may find this next part hard to believe but Nick saw it himself and, as I said, he's a very truthful boy. Besides, if you can believe in rainbow bridges and eight-legged horses, you can believe this.

The messengers went out. The halls of Valhalla emptied and heroes traveled the world, telling everyone they met of Baldur's death and Hela's deal for his return.

And those they told wept. Asgard echoed for the first time with the sobbing of gods and of Valkyrior. In Midgard, men cried in their fields and over their forges. Women cried alone in their homes or together in their villages. Children and babes cried though they didn't know exactly why.

But Asgard and Midgard were filled with more than the tears of men. Dogs howled. Cats screeched. Cows lowed. Rabbits screamed. Birds squawked. Horses neighed. Pigs squealed. Snakes hissed. Frogs croaked. Fish moved their mouths in sorrowful, silent kisses.

The plants mourned Baldur too. On the morning of the fourteenth day, there was a dew on the plants like no one had ever seen. Beads of water formed on every plant until the water rolled from their leaves and dripped to the ground. Even the driest plants in the warmest places squeezed out a drop. Sometimes only a single drop, but that was enough.

Even things that weren't alive wept for Baldur. On the fourteenth day, they all sweat, beading up until water ran down them, just like the inside of a cold window in wintertime. Homes and hearths, tools and torches, swords and scabbards, plates and pictures, wheels and wagons—cool drops of sorrow trickled down them all.

The heroes of Valhalla covered the world. They told Baldur's tragic story to everyone and everything in Asgard and Midgard. And every god, every person, every animal, every plant, every thing wept at the cruel fate that had sent Baldur to Niffleheim.

Except one.

★ ★ ★

As the sun prepared to set on the fourteenth and last day, Nick and Sleipnir skittered to a halt in front of a cave. The dwindling red light made the mouth of the cave seem like, well, a great big, dark mouth. Sleipnir's nostrils widened and he jerked his head to one side. Clip-Clatter-Clop-Clip, he stomped.

"You got that right," said Nick and wrinkled his nose as a stink like warm cheese in a sweaty shoe wafted out of the opening.

After two weeks of non-stop galloping to tell everyone about Baldur, Nick was exhausted. He didn't know why

Hermod had wanted to meet him here at this dark, smelly place but he knew one thing—there was no way he was going in there.

Hermod stepped out of the cave. He was scowling and chewing on his lips beneath his pale blond beard. "Good, you made it," he said. "You've got to come in here."

Nick stared at his friend, who seemed to bring more of the stink out with him. "You're kidding."

"No, I'm not," said Hermod with no trace of a smile. "She won't cry."

Nick didn't notice the cave's smell or darkness anymore. His complete attention was focused on Hermod and the dying light of the setting sun. "What do you mean?" he asked.

"I mean I've told her everything and she refuses to cry. Says she doesn't care." Hermod raised a hand to shade his pale eyes from the red sun. "And we're almost out of time. We can't get the others here fast enough. We have to convince her." He gave a last look at the horizon. "Now."

Nick didn't need to be told twice. With a pat on his mane, Nick slid down Sleipnir's neck and hopped to the ground. "Let's go," he said. Then Hermod guided him into the cave.

The darkness only lasted for a moment. Before they had gone five steps, Nick saw firelight flickering along the rough brown cave walls. With each step, the darkness lessened. Unfortunately, the stink got worse.

"Geez-ow," Nick muttered as the smell grew.

"Aye," murmured Hermod. "Giantesses are not known for their cooking."

They stopped in a cavern hollowed out of earth and rock. Right in the middle, a black pot, as big as Nick, sat on a fire pit. Whatever was in the pot was orange and gooey and bubbled thickly. As each bubble burst, a puff of orange steam rose writhing into the air. When one of the steam clouds passed Nick, he almost puked. That was the source of the smell. He grimaced and shook his head.

"Don't you be likin' my cookin', dearie?" said a cackling voice. "Pity that. I've been at it all day."

Stirring the pot was a giantess. She was square and gray like a cement block. Dirty gray hair hung from her head in long tatters. Her arms and legs were thick as logs. Her face was wizened and warty and filled with deep lines like a dried apple doll. Her eyes were too far apart and when she smiled, she showed off her teeth. All five of them.

"And here old Thaukt went and cooked all day for ye two," the giantess continued. "Not to often poor Thaukt has visitors, no, but when she hears fine handsome heroes are traveling, she makes a special stew, yes she does, to feed the fine hungry men who've been riding so fast and so far in such a terrible hurry." She clucked her tongue and shook her head.

Nick wasn't sure what to pay attention to, the reek of the stew, the criss-crossing wrinkles of her face, or the grating cackle of her voice. A tatter of gray cloth fell off Thaukt's sleeve into the stew. Without seeming to notice, she stirred it right in.

"Mistress Thaukt," said Hermod. "Here is the boy I told you about, Nick Snow. He heard Hela's words with his own ears, like I said."

"Nick Snow, eh? A strange name, a strange name. A Sun Warrior named Snow. Strange indeed." She clucked twice.

"Hello, Mistress Thaukt," said Nick. He wasn't sure what Hermod wanted him to do but he'd told the story often enough over the last fourteen days to be over any shyness about it. "We've come to tell you about Baldur the Good—how he was mistakenly killed and taken to Niffleheim and how Hela will let him return if. . . ."

"Yes, yes, Thaukt knows all that, dearie Snow," croaked Thaukt with a wave of one wrinkled hand. "Herman here told old Thaukt the whole tale, though he had to shout parts. She can't hear so well now."

"Then you know that if everyone cries by tonight, Hela will let Baldur come back to Asgard."

"Yes, yes dearie Snow, your friend Helmut explained it all. Just wanted to meet you Thaukt did."

Relief surged through Nick. They still had time. "So you'll cry for him then?"

"Oh no, no, dearie Snow," the giantess cackled good-naturedly. She stopped stirring and raised her vivid green eyes to Nick for the first time. "Old Thaukt will do no such thing."

The words smacked Nick square in the face, leaving his cheeks hot and flushed.

Nick could almost feel the sun setting outside the cave and knew the day was almost done. Their time and their friend, his friend, would soon be gone.

Though her words knocked the breath out of him, Nick pulled it back in and rushed on. "Please Mistress Thaukt, you have to. Hela said everyone has to or Baldur can't come back and everyone has but you."

The old giantess went back to stirring her pot, her wrinkled face unreadable. "Well dearie Snow, old Thaukt never saw him before so what difference does it make to her if he doesn't come back? He never visited lonely Thaukt in her cave, no he didn't, and there's many a night when she would have liked the company, yes there was. No, Thaukt won't cry for someone she hasn't met, or for his mother or his father or any of his friends, no, no." She clucked, shaking her head each time.

Nick could feel hope sinking with the sun. Until Hermod spoke. "Well if you won't cry for them, will you cry for you?"

The giantess fixed Hermod with a green stare. "Is Hamhocks threatening old Thaukt?"

"No, Mistress," Hermod said. "I'm asking if there's something that you want. That you'll cry for."'

"Dearie, no," said Thaukt. "I have everything I need right here. What could you possible give old Thaukt." She cluckingly shook her head and her face stayed unreadable but Nick thought her green eyes glittered. Just a little.

"Odin will give you whatever you want," continued Hermod. "Just cry for Baldur now and we'll bring Odin back with whatever you ask for."

"No, no," clucked the giantess. "Old Thaukt isn't so stupid, no she isn't. She doesn't trust crafty Odin. If old Thaukt cries now, she'll never see that one-eyed crow-whisperer, no she won't. He'll forget all about old Thaukt once he has what he wants, yes he will. No, old Thaukt is very happy with what she has here in her cave." She began to hum a grating, off-key tune as she stirred her pot.

Nick could almost feel the sun setting outside. "Please," he said. "We'll give you whatever we have."

The giantess whirled on Nick and fixed him with that green stare. "Will you now, dearie Snow?" she said quickly. "And what might ye have that an old giantess would want?"

Suddenly, Nick felt very uncomfortable. He had two valuable things with him. And he had a strong feeling that he shouldn't lose either of them.

The giantess stared at him hungrily. Waiting. "What do you have for old Thaukt," she said again.

Nick put a hand in his pocket. He had a strong feeling that he shouldn't pull it out. He had a stronger one that he had to free Baldur.

"Just these," he said. And he pulled out his deck of cards.

With surprising agility for an old giantess, Thaukt skipped around the pot to stand before Nick. "What are these, dearie?" said Thaukt gleefully.

"Cards, Mistress Thaukt. Special cards." He fanned them out so she could see.

Thaukt's green eyes sparkled. "Pictures. Some have pictures now. And what do they do, dearie Snow?"

"They have pictures of people here and tell you about them." He saw Thaukt's face fall a bit and realized that that wasn't a very convincing reason to take the cards. "And sometimes they tell you what could happen or help you solve a mystery about what has happened. And look," he held up a blank card, "new ones appear all the time."

From the skeptical look on her face, Nick saw he'd have to show her.Nick thought about people he'd met but whose name he had not said. He knew Thaukt wasn't in here because he'd said her name and nothing had happened. He frantically thought until a name, an obvious name, popped into his head. A name he hadn't said because he'd tried to forget it.

"Fenris Wolf," said Nick. They waited.

The deck vibrated. Nick saw the picture appear on the card—a black wolf howling at the sky, bound to a rainbow by a thin gold chain. Nick shuddered when he saw it.

Now Thaukt's face was positively greedy. Her eyes shone and she began to rub her hands on her gray sack of a dress. "Let us see, dearie," she gulped.

Reluctantly, Nick held the card closer to Thaukt. She stared, her green eyes scanning the card from side to side. "We can't read it," Nick heard her whisper. "We still can't read it." Louder, she said, "What does it say, dearie?"

Nick read it aloud:

The Fenris Wolf guards the rainbow bridge, bound by the Gleipnir chain. Add 10 to his attack if his father Loki is also on the field."

Looking at the picture reminded Nick of the wolf's piercing howl and its awful yellow eyes. Nick tried to suppress a shudder he couldn't help.

"Ah dearie Snow, only a brave man can pass the wolf," she said. "What's a card to that, eh?" She wheedled closer to him until Nick could smell her rotten breath.

"Give them to me, dearie," she said softly. "Old Thaukt will take them, yes she will."

Nick had an unshakable feeling he was doing something wrong but he couldn't think of any other way to get his friend back. He looked at Hermod for guidance but the Norseman just shrugged. Great, Nick thought. Let the kid make the decisions.

"Will you cry?" Nick asked.

"The cards first, dearie Snow, the cards first. Then old Thaukt will cry."

Still not sure he was doing the right thing but unable to think of anything else to free his friend, Nick held out the card. The giantess reached a gnarled hand out to take it. Nick thought her mouth was actually starting to water.

As her fingers touched the card, Thaukt screamed. And not a dainty "oh that startled me" scream but a "Odin's Beard my hand is on fire" sort of scream. She whipped her hand back and the card fell to the floor. Nick looked at her, uncertain what to do.

"I can't touch it," she shrieked. "I still can't touch it." She seemed hurt and angry and disappointed and somehow, the way all of these emotions came to rest in her dried face, made her seem scarier than ever.

"These are no good to Thaukt, dearie Snow, no good at all. What can old Thaukt do with cards she can't read or touch." She fairly spit that last sentence. "No, no good at all." The old giantess clucked furiously and returned to her pot. She stirred, slowly shaking her head. Gradually, she seemed to calm as she muttered. "No use. No use at all."

Nick saw his only hope for Baldur drifting away like the dropped card. As he picked up the Fenris Wolf card, he realized he had one other thing to offer her. He flexed his arm and felt the tightness of the armring. But he dismissed the idea of offering her the armring almost as soon as he thought of it. Baldur would never, ever forgive him if he gave the armring to a giant. Even to save him.

Nick had nothing else to give the giantess. "Mistress Thaukt," he said finally. "Please. He's the best friend I've had here, my first one. Please let me see him again." The thought of Baldur trapped in Hela's cold banquet hall seemed very real to Nick right then and he choked a little, fighting a tear of his own.

The old giantess stared at Nick, those vivid green eyes glittering out of the wrinkled, unreadable face. "Now, now dearie Snow, hasn't there been enough of that? No more tears. A boy like you with gods for friends and magic cards shouldn't be crying. You'll have other best friends. Why, Herring here seems like a wonderful fellow. Old Thaukt doesn't have any friends, no she doesn't, and you don't see her crying in her stew pot, no you don't. No, no dearie Snow, Thaukt thinks there've been too many tears. The time for that is done, yes it is."

Nick knew the time was just about gone. "Please," he said. "Please."

Her green eyes stayed cold. "No, dearie Snow. No indeed." She put down her stirring spoon, which was the size of an oar, and reached into the pot with at bucket-sized ladle. She slopped some stew into a bowl and held the stinking goo out to Nick. "Have some stew, dearie Snow?"

"No, thank you," Nick said. "But please Mistress Thaukt, if you'd only . . ."

Thaukt clucked rapidly and shook her head. "Old Thaukt is hungry, yes she is. She's been cooking all day she has and she's ready to eat. Now dearie Snow and Heckler will join Thaukt or they'll leave they will, for the time to talk is gone and the time to eat is come."

She stood, holding out the stinking bowl with her dirty, wrinkled hands. Her cold green eyes and wizened face made it hard for Nick to tell what she was thinking. But he saw one thing.

There was not a tear in her.

"We must leave, Mistress Thaukt," Nick choked. "Thank you for the offer," the ever polite boy said.

"If you must, dearie Snow, if you must. Good-bye and good fortune to you. Old Thaukt hopes you find your way home with those cards of yours, yes she does. And soon too. And farewell to you Huckleberry."

Hermod put a hand on Nick's shoulder and the two walked back toward the cave entrance. The only relief they felt was that the stench faded as they left Thaukt's chamber. Finally, they stepped back outside, into the cool, clean air.

It was dark.

Chapter 15

"Where is she?" bellowed Odin. He smashed his shield so hard against the mountainside that it shook the ground. "Where is the foul hag?! Where is the tearless crone who doomed my son?!"

After they had left Thaukt's cave, Nick, Sleipnir, and Hermod had returned to Asgard to tell Frigga and Odin about the giantess who refused to cry. The two gods weren't surprised by Nick's tale since Baldur hadn't returned and because (Nick suspected) Hugin and Munin had already told Odin what had happened. Even though it had been too late to save Baldur, Odin had demanded that Nick and Hermod lead him to the cave so he could meet the giantess himself. Young as he was, even Nick could tell it wasn't to talk things over. When they had reached the cave, Odin's control had burst.

So now the All-Father was swinging his shield against the mountain, yelling for Thaukt to come out. Hugin and Munin flapped on his shoulders, riding the wind of his anger. Freki and Geri joined Odin's bellows with howls that bared their white fangs.

"Serpent's Teeth!" swore Odin. "Come OUT!"

There was no answer from the cave. If there had, Nick was pretty sure he would have learned what a smithereen looked like.

Nick peered out from around Sleipnir's lowered head (they'd both ducked on Odin's last blast). "She was inside, Mr. Odin," he volunteered. A little extra courtesy seemed like the smart idea just then.

"Then bring her out here," Odin roared. "Freki! Geri!"

The wolves shot into the cave as if they'd been released from an invisible leash. More growls echoed back to them as Odin impatiently tapped the butt of his spear on the ground. The growls tapered off into inquisitive barks, the same sort of bark Nick's dog Joe made when he was looking for a chew toy (usually the purple squeaky one).

"By the Horn!" yelled Odin. "If I have to come in there and find her with one eye . . ."

A high pitched bark cut Odin off.

"That's it!" Odin barked himself and stomped into the cave. Hermod waved Nick in and hurried after Odin. Nick followed.

Nick ran down the passage to the chamber where he'd met Thaukt the night before. In the light of the dying flames in the center of the floor, Nick saw Freki and Geri circling the rough hewn room, sniffing around the edges of the stone walls. Odin stood with his hands on hips, his tall helmet barely clearing the ceiling. The god filled up the entire center of the room. He was so big in fact, that it took Nick a moment to figure out what was different.

Everything was gone.

The rough hewn table in the back. The lamps hanging from the walls. The filthy bed. The great black pot that had been filled with the goop stew. Even the reek of the stew which Nick thought would never leave his clothes. It was all gone. Only the last embers of the fire remained and those were swiftly turning to ash.

"She didn't have time to move all this," Hermod said.

"Especially not the stink," said Nick.

"You're sure this is the cave?" asked Odin through clenched teeth.

"I know it is," nodded Hermod, "because I found her here first but she wouldn't listen to me so I went and got Nick and brought him back in to help me and we stood right where you are only there was a big black stew pot between us and Nick tried to convince her to cry like everyone else but she wouldn't so Nick offered her his cards and she reached out to take a card but it hurt her or stung her or something because she snatched her hand back and yelled that she still couldn't touch it and the card fell to the floor right where you're standing until Nick picked it up . . ."

"Enough!" bellowed Odin. "Then where is the hag now?!"

"Wait!" Nick interrupted. Odin whirled on him, his eye blazing. Nick ignored him (Yikes!) and turned to his friend. "Hermod! She said 'I *still* can't touch it?'"

Hermod blinked. "Sure, Nick. Don't you remember?"

"I do," Nick nodded. "But this was the first time I'd seen her. How could she have tried to touch them *before?*"

Hermod blinked some more. "I don't know," he said.

"I held out the Fenris Wolf card," Nick said, remembering. "And I shuddered because it reminded me of the real thing and she said 'What's a card to the real thing? Only a brave man can pass the wolf.'" Another thought hit Nick. "And how did she know I passed Fenris Wolf?"

Nick had Odin's attention. "Who else would know?" the All-Father asked.

"Both of you," said Nick, thinking. "Baldur. Frigga. Heimdall." Nick stopped as he remembered another conversation in Valhalla.

"Loki."

"Loki?!" Odin rumbled ominously.

"At your feast when I was eating with Baldur. Loki sat down and said Fenris Wolf had told him that I was brave when I passed."

"So Loki tried to touch the cards at the banquet?" Odin asked.

"No," said Nick, shaking his head. "He didn't seem to know about them."

"Who has tried to touch them?" Odin asked.

Nick combed his memory for every possible person. There was only one. "King Thrym. He tried to touch them and pulled his hand away like they stung him." He paused as things began to make sense. "Just like Thaukt."

"You saw old Thrym?" asked Odin in surprise. "When?"

"Right when I got here. He saved me from one of his giants and then almost ate me himself. Baldur stopped him."

"How long was that before you came to Valhalla?"

Nick thought. "About a day."

"Then it couldn't have been Thrym," said Odin, shaking his head.

"Why not?" asked Nick. "Baldur said it was."

"Because Thrym was with me," said Odin.

"With you?" asked Hermod with surprise in his voice now. "What were you doing?"

"Fighting," said Odin.

"Are you sure?" asked Hermod.

"A giant king swinging an ax at your head tends to leave an impression," said Odin.

"Then who was with me?" asked Nick.

"Someone who wanted the first shot at your cards," said Odin. "But didn't want anyone to know it." Hugin squawked. "Someone who can change forms."

"Loki," said Nick, remembering what Baldur had told him in the underworld. "Loki wants the cards. It's got to be him."

"But why?" Odin rumbled.

Nick shook his head, preoccupied with sorting through his encounters with Loki. Both the giant king and the giantess had been Loki in disguise. He'd apparently met the god of mischief in his true form at the banquet in Valhalla. And Loki must have been talking to his children since he knew Nick had passed the wolf and Hela knew Loki was looking for the cards. It all made Nick's head spin. Judging from the silence, Hermod and Odin (and Hugin and Munin) were trying to wrap their heads around it too.

"Maybe Loki's card tells us something about what he's doing," said Hermod.

"Or he's afraid of what it says," offered Odin.

Remembering how the Baldur card and the Hermod card had given them clues about what was going on, Nick jammed his hand into his pocket and pulled out the deck. He fanned through the cards until he found Loki, a shadowy-faced man standing on the rainbow between Odin and the giants. Hermod stood next to Nick and Odin loomed behind him as he read the description aloud:

> *The god of mischief straddles the realms of gods and giants in Asgard and Jotunheim. With Loki on the field, add 10 to the attacks of Fenris Wolf, the Midgard Serpent, and Hela, his children.*

All three (seven counting crows and wolves) were silent.

"Well that doesn't help us at all," said Nick finally.

"True," said Odin. "But none of us can read it."

"So?" said Nick, not understanding why that mattered.

"So Loki doesn't know what it says. Or that it doesn't help us."

Hermod looked up at Odin. "So is he up to something, Father?"

"It's Loki," scoffed Odin. "Of course he's up to something."

"But what?" asked Nick.

"I don't know," said Odin. "But we've discovered something more important."

Nick looked up at Odin. The god's white beard bristled and his single eye blazed with anger. "Loki was the giantess in disguise. Which means that the Trickster killed my son by fooling a blind man and then kept him from coming back by refusing to cry."

Odin took the point of his spear and twirled it between his thumb and forefinger. He curled his lips in the most maliciously intense grin Nick would ever see.

"It's time to find Loki. And give him something to cry about."

As soon as they left the cave, Odin sent Hugin and Munin to search for Loki. When the crows had dwindled to black dots in the clouds, he sent Freki and Geri back to Valhalla to tell Frigga what Loki had done and to relay his order to send the gods and heroes out in search of the god of mischief. Then the fierce chieftain of the Norse gods stalked into the mountains himself, muttering about fake giantesses, frozen goddesses, and hidden plots.

Nick and Hermod quickly climbed onto Sleipnir and followed Odin into the mountains. A day later, they were still following him. The All-Father refused to stop for woods or streams or peaks or valleys or cold or food or even sleep. Nick was never more glad to have Sleipnir because he knew he'd never have been able to keep up with the angry Norse god without him. Fast as he was though, Sleipnir was careful to stay behind Odin, which seemed like a good idea to Nick given the way Odin was stalking and growling the whole time. When Odin started snapping trees as he walked, purely out of distracted anger, it seemed like a great idea.

Hugin and Munin flew back and forth constantly, sometimes together, sometimes apart. One (or both) would land on Odin's shoulder and whisper in his ear (which still gave Nick the heebie-jeebies). Sometimes Odin continued straight ahead and sometimes he changed direction but he always cursed Loki when he did it.

It was the middle of the morning on the next day when both crows landed on Odin's shoulders. Their squawking chatter woke Nick, who had once again fallen asleep on Sleepnir's back. Hugin and Munin weren't whispering this time. They were shrieking and squawking and batting their wings so fiercely that Odin had to stop. As Sleipnir trotted up next to Odin, Nick saw the All-Father listening intently to the crows, bent slightly forward, his one eye squinted in concentration.

With one last shriek, the crows stopped and Odin's eye widened. "We've got him then!" For the first time since they'd set out, Odin looked at Hermod and Nick. He grinned ferociously and said, "A fishing village! Who would have thought of a fishing village?! He hates fish!" Then Odin turned west and sprinted off, the crows flapping on his shoulders and squawking encouragement.

"I don't think he's going to wait for us," said Nick.

"Nope," said Hermod.

Clip-clip-clap-clip, stomped Sleipnir in agreement, and galloped after the All-Father.

Three cottages hardly seemed like a village to Nick. Made of gray stone with thatched roofs, the cottages sat in a small row along a wide, clear river that tumbled and frothed over dark, smooth rocks. By the time Nick and Hermod arrived, Odin was barreling out of one cottage and bursting into a second.

"Come out, Trickster!" he yelled. "The crows saw you! Said you've been hiding as a fisherman! Might have fooled them too except you changed back to your real shape last night when you thought no one was watching."

Odin kept shouting as he exited the second cottage and headed into the third. "Your fire's still warm, Loki! You haven't been gone long! You're close enough to hear me! I know you can hear me! Come out, Loki! Come explain why you killed my son! Then explain why you kept him from coming back! And then you can explain to me why I shouldn't spit you with my spear!"

"Think he'll answer?" asked Hermod with a smile.

"Only if he's tired of the way he's put together," Nick replied.

Odin came out of the last cottage, his chest heaving. Nick thought it looked more like anger than exertion. "They're all empty!" he spat. "There's nothing here."

The crows squawked in unison.

"Well look!" Odin scowled. "He's obviously not here now."

The crows squawked again. "Fine," Odin said in disgust. He turned to Hermod and Nick. "They swear he's here but I haven't seen a thing. Take another look in the cottages. I'm going to look in the woods." Without waiting for an answer, Odin stomped into the pine forest, snapping the top of a tree as he went.

Nick eyed the tree. "I think we should hurry."

"Good idea," said Hermod.

Nick hopped off Sleipnir (he'd become quite a horseman over the last two weeks) and went from cottage to cottage with Hermod. Each cottage only had one room so there really weren't many places for a largish god of mischief to hide. They checked under the beds (there was one in each cottage), in the fireplaces (same thing), in a trunk (middle cottage) and in the outhouse (which the cottages must have shared). They found nothing.

After they'd searched the cottages, they went down to the river. A shallow fishing boat was tied to a wooden dock that was so old it was gray. A tall, thin shed stood at the edge of the dock, listing to one side as if it could collapse at any moment. Nick opened its battered wooden door and peaked inside. It was filled with supplies. Coils of rope, buckets of tar (some with brushes still stuck to them), and nets and nets and nets and nets that hung from hooks on the walls or lay piled on the floor. Fishing supplies, Nick thought, and started to shut the door. Then the net caught his eye.

A net hung from the ceiling that was altogether different from the others. It wasn't frayed, it didn't stink, and there wasn't a single broken mesh. No, this net was whole and fine and shimmered silvery in the dim light of the shed. Nick put a hand behind it so that it fell over his fingers. It rested lightly, like a cobweb. But when Nick grabbed it with both hands and pulled, he grimaced in pain and surprise as the thin fibers dug deep into his skin. Though his fishing experience was limited to poles, Nick knew right away that no fish was escaping from this net.

He slipped it off the hook and carried it out with him. "What'd you find?" Hermod asked as Nick emerged.

"A net," said Nick, still playing with it.

"There must be dozens of them," said Hermod.

"Not like this," Nick replied.

Hermod held it up to the sun with the practiced eye of someone who knew what he was looking at, which Nick knew to be true (you don't travel for almost three weeks with someone without hearing about his love of fishing). "This is amazing," Hermod said with a reverence you normally heard only in church.

"Yeah?" said Nick.

"Look at the mesh, how fine it is." He put one hand against the net. "There has to be 50, 55 squares to a palm here. Yet it's so flexible. You can't make something this flexible out of metal, it just won't bend like this." He flexed it back and forth to demonstrate. "It's moves as free as twine. But it's so much stronger. And these weights," he ran a hand along the silver teardrop-shaped weights that ran all around the edges. "Perfectly balanced. Perfectly spaced." He sighed and then, in an incredible display of his admiration for the net, stopped talking.

Nick didn't really get what Hermod was so excited about. "Is it really such a big deal?"

Hermod ran his hand along the net again. "A fisherman spends as much time mending his nets as fishing with them. With a net like this," he shook his head. "You'd catch twice the fish in half the time."

Nick had just about run out of net conversation when Odin rejoined them, splashing through the river as he waded over through thigh-deep water. Judging from his bristling white beard and his scowling blue eye, he was not happy.

"He's not here," Odin spat. "If he ever was."

Hugin and Munin squawked at the same time.

"Look around you two! There's no sign of him!"

This time Hugin and Munin cackled and flapped their wings.

"No, I'm not some great all-seeing crow but I can spot a Trickster when I have to and he's not here."

The two crows actually jumped up and down on Odin's shoulders, screamed, and beat their wings like drums. "Fine," Odin said. "He was here. But he's not now." That was apparently as much as Odin was willing to argue with birds because he then turned to Nick and Hermod, and Sleipnir, who had trotted down to join them. "Find anything?" he asked gruffly.

"We searched all three cottages," said Hermod, shaking his head. "And we checked the trunk and the outhouse and the shed but we didn't find anything except this net which isn't Loki but it's really something because it's light and flexible and strong and I can't believe how small this mesh is because I've fished all my life and I've never seen anything like it even from Frey and he knows his fishing so I can't imagine who could have made something so fine and clever . . ."

"Is it the cleverest net you've ever seen?" Odin interrupted.

Hermod blinked. Twice. "Yes," he said.

"Then it's Loki's net. He was here."

Hugin and Munin cawed.

"Oh, shut it," said Odin.

"How do you know it's Loki's net?" Nick broke in.

"I want to twist Loki to bits," said Odin. "But if something is the cleverest you've ever seen, he probably did it. The net's his."

Suddenly, Nick's pocket began to vibrate.

They all heard the faint buzzing. The others went still as Nick slapped his hand into his pocket and pulled out the blue deck. Nick quickly ran through the cards, searching for a new one. He thumbed past Odin and Frigga, past Hunin and Baldur, past Fenris Wolf until. . . .

"Loki's Net!" Nick yelled, and held up the new card.

"Whatsitsay?" asked Odin and Hermod at the same time.

Nick turned the card back to him. A black net was pictured in front of blue water. He read the card out loud:

> *After he killed Baldur, Loki hid from the angry gods as a fisherman. When the gods closed in, Loki turned into a fish.*

Nick looked up at Odin with a grin that was as fearsome and ferocious as the All-Father's own as he read the rest:

> *Odin then caught him with his own net.*

Odin's eye blazed and his beard bristled as he realized what Nick had said. "We're goin' fishin' boys," he yelled and held out a hand for the net. When Hermod tossed it to him, Odin snatched the net out of the air, and in one smooth motion, turned and whirled it into the river.

Odin grinned. "And we're fryin' what we catch."

Chapter 16

Nick watched the net sail across the river, spinning through the air and spreading out flatly like one of the giant stingrays he saw in the ocean near his grandma's home. The net ripped smoothly into the water, as if it were designed to slice straight down to where the fish were hiding.

Hermod sighed as Odin pulled the net effortlessly through the water. Nick could see from the way his big friend's hands twitched that he was itching to join Odin and take a cast himself.

But it was equally clear that Odin wasn't about to give it up. The Ruler of the Gods cast the net with methodical intensity, moving from one shore of the river to the other and back again, and neither Nick nor Hermod were going to interrupt him. Each time Odin pulled the net out, it was filled with fish (Nick didn't know enough about Norse fish to know what they were but he thought he recognized a trout or two). Each time, Odin held the net up and stared at the fish wriggling inside. Most of the time, he opened the net right away and threw them all back. Twice, he brought the net to shore and spread his catch on the ground, staring intently at dozens of flopping fish. Nick didn't know what he was looking for (a "Hi, I'm Loki" name tag didn't seem too likely) but both times, Odin picked up the fish and tossed them back.

Odin had gone back and forth across the main section of the river twice when he stood up straight and placed his hands on his hips. His single eye focused intently on the water, scanning from one side to the other. Again, Nick didn't know what Odin was looking for. Judging from the crows' unusual silence, they didn't either.

But Hermod did. "The log," whispered Hermod. "If I were a fish, I'd hide under the log."

Odin turned slightly to his right. There Nick saw a huge old tree trunk that had fallen from their side of the bank into the water. Half-rotted with a gaping hole in its center, the trunk stretched at least twenty feet into the river, blocking the current so that the water behind it was calm and still and shaded. A few cat-tails from the bank extended down into the still water.

Fish heaven.

Odin didn't seem to notice Hermod's suggestion and cast the net into the middle of the river again. As Odin pulled the net back in, his back was still turned to the tree trunk. "Nothing," he said as he lifted the empty net. He stared in disappointment at the fish-free mesh and took two innocent seeming steps backwards. Then he looked right at Nick with his one eye.

And winked.

Before Nick knew what was happening, Odin whirled and leapt for the tree trunk. With blurring speed, Odin grabbed the old log with one hand and whipped the net underneath it with the other. As soon as it sliced all the way into the water, Odin yanked it back out like a yo-yo. Whatever was in the net thrashed and sent foam splashing into the air. Odin yelled and wrapped both hands around the net and high-stepped to shore, holding the wildly wriggling net out in front of him. With a second yell, so sharp and so loud that Nick thought his ears would pop, Odin slammed the net on the bank, pounded it with his fist twice, and pulled out a large, pink, and rather stunned-looking, fish.

Nick barely had time to notice the fish's pink and blue scales shimmering in the sun, or the way its body was flattened by Odin's great grip, or the silent, frantic kissing motion of its mouth (although the little he saw obviously made enough of an impression that he remembered to tell us about it), because the next moment, Odin's hands weren't wrapped around a fish. They were wrapped around the neck of a red-headed, red-faced, thrashing, gasping, extremely panicked-looking man. Though he'd only met him once (in this form anyway), Nick recognized him immediately.

Loki.

Of course, Nick remembered Valhalla-Loki, the smooth, sarcastic god with a smart-aleck, self-satisfied expression on his face. Choking-Loki, on the other hand, was a wet, dirty mess whose green eyes bugged out of his head as Odin squeezed his neck with both hands.

Pinned to his back, Loki grabbed the dirt and rocks on the bank and flung them wildly in every direction. Odin just laughed as the rocks pelted off his helmet and breastplate. "Is that all you have, Trickster? Can't you throw any harder? You have an arm like a wet wheat stalk!"

Loki kicked and threw even harder and seemed to panic but now the rocks flew in a new direction. At Nick.

"Geezow!" yelped Nick. He ducked his head, raised his arms, jumped to the side and twisted but he couldn't avoid the shower of stones. A god, especially a strangling, angry one, can throw pretty fast. Unable to get out of the way, Nick covered his head with his hands and cringed as he waited for the stones to brain him. And waited. And waited.

When nothing happened, Nick raised his head to see the stones coming straight for him, just as fast as Loki could throw them. Nick winced and ducked again but he still wasn't hit. Then he heard the clatter of stones around him and looked back up, not quite believing what he saw.

The stones were still coming straight for him but at the last second, and not more than a few inches away, they bounced to the side like he was wearing a force field. Nick put one hand up to the armband and felt its cool metal. It worked. The armband worked, just like Baldur said it would. The rocks wouldn't hit him, just like they'd promised Frigga.

Now Nick had seen this happen often enough with Baldur but it was a totally different experience when the missiles were flying at him. He flinched a few more times as the rocks whizzed by so close that he could feel the air whoosh on his face. As he got used to it though, he started to laugh. He waved one hand and saw a rock curve twice to avoid hitting it. He started to jump at the rocks, forcing them to bend away. He laughed louder now, totally unafraid of rocks that would have smashed his skull. If they could hit him.

Odin slackened his strangling to look back and see what was going on. When he saw, he started laughing too. Then he turned back to Loki. "Stop that!" he snapped. Loki kept throwing, his face as red as his hair. Odin began to pound Loki's head rhythmically against the ground in time with his words. "I-said-stop-that-Trick-ster. I'd-pound-your-head-all-day-but-I'll-get-bored-and-you'll-get-a-very-very-very-very-very-bad-headache." On "headache," Odin lifted Loki half off the ground and gave him one last big crack. The rocks stopped and Loki went still. Odin picked him up again and Loki's head lolled back, limp. "Humphf," Odin said. Then he smashed Loki's head against the dirt one more time for good measure.

"He'll be out for awhile," said Odin with a satisfied grin.

"You can knock out gods?" asked Nick.

Odin raised one eyebrow. "Who do you think you're talking to?"

"True," said Nick.

Odin reached into a pouch at his belt and pulled out a small, thin, gold chain. He set Loki up against a tree and quickly bound him with the chain. "He shouldn't wake up," Odin said as he worked. "But if he does, this should hold him."

"It looks awfully small," said Nick.

"It's part of the Gleipnir chain. I kept the extra links we didn't need." He finished tying Loki. "For something exactly like this."

"Why are you tying him?"

"So he won't get away while I'm gone."

Nick's mouth wouldn't work. "Gone?" was all he could say.

"I'm planning something special for the man who killed my son. It'll take a little extra work. I'm going to set it up and then I'll be back."

"But what if he wakes up?" asked Nick starting to panic. Just Hermod and him? With a god called the Trickster?

"Then he'll be bound by an unbreakable chain and you'll be wearing an armring that makes you invulnerable." Odin squinted intently at Nick. "That is what just happened, isn't it?"

Nick didn't see any point in lying to Odin since the god had seen the rocks bounce away. He nodded.

"Then what's there to worry about?" asked Odin. "Just don't listen to him and everything will be fine."

Nick didn't like the sound of this at all but Odin didn't seem to care. He gave the chain one last tug and started to walk away, quickly.

"Wait," yelled Nick. "How long will it take?"

"A few hours. You'll be fine. We'll be done by supper. Now take care of him. Hermod will help you."

"But what if he . . ." Nick trailed off. Odin was already gone. Nick looked from the unconscious, bound god of mischief to Hermod. "What are we going to do?"

"What are you worried about?" said Hermod. "You're invulnerable. I'm the one who should be worried."

"Fair enough," Nick said, realizing the truth of it. "Well then, let's wait," he said, and sat down, facing the unconscious Loki. Hermod joined him. And they waited.

Invulnerable, Nick thought. With Baldur's armring on, nothing could hurt him. Nothing in the world. Except mistletoe he supposed. But since he knew what that looked like, he'd be sure to avoid it. Especially spears of it.

Anyway, if nothing could hurt him, then he didn't have to be afraid. Not of giants or wolves or spears or rocks. Or even gods of mischief. Not with the armring. Not ever again.

As Nick sat watching Loki, he ran his hand around the band, spinning it around his thin arm, now used to its weight and how it fit, no longer amazed that it hugged his thin arm as well as it had Baldur's massive one. He couldn't feel its magic or Frigga's promise but he also couldn't feel any fear of being hurt and that lack of feeling was more incredible than any magic one.

Nothing can hurt me, Nick thought as he stared at Loki. Not even the god of mischief himself. Of course that didn't seem like much of a problem anymore as the Trickster lay chained against the tree, his head lolling to the side, his eyes closed, and his mouth open.

"I'm thirsty," said Nick, realizing it had been sometime since Odin had left.

"Stream's over there," said Hermod, pointing.

Nick sighed. Drinking all this water was starting to wear on him. The first thing he was going to do when he got home was slam a mega-sized sports drink. Sighing again, he trudged over to the stream and filled his hands, slurping the water. He had to admit that it was cool and clear and, at that moment, tasted better than any soda. But not better than a sports drink.

He took one more slurp, shook off his hands, then returned to Hermod and sat down, crossing his legs. He rested his elbow on his knee and put his chin in his hand. He sighed again and looked at Loki.

Loki looked back.

The Trickster was wide awake now, staring at Nick with those green eyes, green eyes he now recognized as Loki's, and Thrym's, and Thaukt's. There was no blood on him and he seemed awfully alert for a guy who'd just had his head smashed in by the ruler of the gods.

Nick gasped and scrambled to his feet. Instinctively, he grabbed the armring and stepped back several steps.

"I can't take it," said Loki matter-of-factly. "And if I can't take it, I can't hurt you."

Nick turned to Hermod for help but his big Norse friend was stretched out on the ground, sleeping. He whirled back on Loki.

The god of mischief smirked. "He," Loki said, nodding at Hermod, "is a different story."

"What did you do?!" Nick yelled, forgetting he was afraid.

"Nothing," said Loki, still smirking. "He slipped."

Nick rushed over to Hermod. His friend was out cold. Nick shook Hermod, then slapped Hermod's face lightly. Nothing.

"He'll be fine," said Loki. "You can't kill a god so easily. I should know."

Sleipnir, Nick thought, and whirled around looking for the faithful, strong, and remarkably intelligent horse.

"Looks like Old Eight Hooves has wandered off," said Loki as if reading his mind. "I think I may have seen a glimpse of a very attractive mare. With eight legs. Quite rare I understand."

You can't hang around with Norse gods for a few weeks without picking up a few choice words. Nick chose a couple. Loki laughed.

Nick was only eleven but he'd now seen an awful lot of different kinds of dangers. And though he couldn't see it, he sure sensed one here now. Even with Loki in chains.

"You did this," accused Nick.

"How could I?" asked Loki and rattled the light gold chain. "I'm chained up. It looks weak, but my son has been yanking at his for years and it still hasn't broken." Loki made a show of examining the chain. "I think it's the bird spit that does it."

Nick started to back away from the bound god. Then he realized that if he did, he would leave Hermod, unconscious and helpless, before the god of mischief. If you've learned nothing else about Nick, you know that he's a loyal friend. So he stopped, sat down next to Hermod, and placed one hand on his felled friend's shoulder.

"Well isn't this nice," said Loki. "We finally have a chance to visit."

"I'm not supposed to talk to you by myself," said Nick quickly.

"Then we'd never get to talk at all," said Loki easily. "You saw how irritated Old One Eye gets with me sometimes. And Mr. Nimble Pants here is always interrupting. No, I think this is the only way we'd get to have an actual conversation."

"Why would you want to talk to me?" asked Nick, wanting to move away but unable to move Hermod.

"Why because you're you of course," Loki replied, still looking at the chain. "You're Nick Snow, the Sun Warrior and the Card Keeper, the Wolf Passer and Gate Jumper, the man who went to Hel for his friend and returned with the armring Drystil." Loki paused and looked up at Nick, his green eyes glittering. "You met my daughter, Hela, didn't you? Tall, striking woman? Half-blue?"

Nick nodded.

"Didn't stare at the blue side, did you?"

Nick shook his head.

"Good, that drives her nuts." Loki smiled. "No, I've been looking forward to talking with you, the boy who read the future in his cards and caught the god of mischief himself."

"Odin caught you. I didn't."

Loki scoffed. "Old One-Eye would still be looking if it weren't for you. And I'd have broken free of any net but mine. Which I believe you gave to him."

Nick's curiosity overcame his fear for a moment. "Why'd you do that anyway? Make such a good net?"

Loki shrugged. "If something is worth doing, it's worth doing right." He looked back at the river. "Besides, I was hungry."

Nick stared at Loki. Loki stared at the river. The river gurgled. A minute went by. It seemed like a very long time to Nick.

"So you've got a magic armring, won Odin's favor, and captured me," Loki said at last. "What's next for the heroic Sun Warrior."

"I need to find my way home," said Nick without thinking. And immediately wished he hadn't.

"Of course," said Loki easily. "Now that you've done all of One-Eye's dirty work, I'm sure he'll send you home."

"He doesn't know how," said Nick.

"Doesn't he?" said Loki, his green eyes dancing. "Interesting."

"What do you mean?"

"I mean I think it's interesting that the All-Father, the Ruler of the Gods, and the Lord of Valhalla doesn't know how to send you home."

"Why?"

"Because I do."

Chapter 17

"How?" Nick blurted before he could stop himself.

"Oh, it's not hard," said Loki, tilting his head casually to the side. "I'm sure Odin will tell you." He flipped his red hair back out of his eyes. "Eventually."

Nick finally remembered Odin's advice and stopped talking. But he couldn't stop himself from listening. Loki was talking about home after all.

"Oh, One-Eye knows. You've seen those crows sitting on his shoulders, whispering, whispering, all the time whispering." Loki shuddered. "It gives me the creeps."

Before he knew it, Nick shuddered right along with him.

"How could he not know? Those infernal crows see everything, even hidden gods. And those wolves, Freeki and Geeki, that are always running around his feet, chewing furniture and messing in the banquet hall. They hear everything; they're just not as showy as those crows when they tell Odin about it. Oh, he knows, you can be sure," Loki finished and smiled that smirking half-smile. "He's just not telling you."

"That's not true!" Nick yelled instinctively.

"Of course it isn't," said Loki calmly.

"Frigga and Odin will send me back as soon as they can!"

"Of course they will Sun Warrior. I'm sure they'll do it just the moment they have a chance. I can hear them now. 'We'll send you right back, Sun Warrior, as soon as we figure out how. But first we need you to take a quick run down to the underworld to get my son. And then, if you don't mind, just hustle on back with a magic armring. But of course, Baldur gave the armring to you and not back to us so if you don't mind, could you just go travel the world and ask every living thing to weep so our little Baldur can return and give the armring back to us. Oh, and one nasty giantess won't cry so do be a dear and talk her into crying for our son—don't worry, she almost never eats children. Then of course you know that that nasty Trickster Loki is behind the whole evil thing and it's really his fault you're still here so would you mind searching for him, figure out where he's hiding, find what I need to catch him, and then guard him while I skitter off the first chance I get? Yes I know you're young and home-sick but it's really just a few small favors isn't it, and what are a few small favors compared to our sending you home? Which we'll do just as soon as you count the snowflakes on the mountainside. And steal Skrymir's Wallet. And run the giants out of Jotunheim. Yes, I'm certain after you do all that we'll just about have it figured out.'"

Loki shook his head. "C'mon, Sun Warrior. They could have sent you back a long time ago." His green eyes softened kindly in sympathy. "They just didn't want to."

Nick didn't know why but that almost made him cry. Of course, it's easy for you and me to see why that would upset him so much—to hear something that sounds so mean that you don't want to believe it but has so much truth in it that it's hard to deny. And before you yell, "BUT HE'S THE GOD OF MISCHIEF FOR PETE'S SAKE!" remember that Nick was tired and alone and hearing it directly from the Trickster himself. I don't know many eleven-year-olds who have stood up to a god with bad intentions so if you ask me, Nick was doing pretty well, all things considered.

"You're lying," Nick coughed.

"Believe me or not," said Loki as casually as one can when chained to a tree. "All I'm saying is that I know how to get you home and I'm not one of the grand high muckety-mucks of Asgard. And if I know, they know."

"Why would they wait?" asked Nick, knowing he should stop but unable to help himself.

"Because they're using you."

"That's not true," Nick whispered. But he desperately, desperately feared it was.

"Really?" said Loki, seemingly unaware of Nick's welling-eyes. "Why did they send you to Niffleheim? Are children sent to the underworld so often in your land? Think how many other people they could have sent instead of you. Why didn't they send another one of their sons? Because they'd lost one already. Why not a hero from that hall of theirs? Because they can't afford to lose a single one for Ragnarok. How about Old One-Eye himself? No, that would've required him to pull his royal butt off his comfy golden throne."

"No, no, it's far easier to send a strange boy from a strange land into danger. Better to lose a Sun Warrior no one knows than a hero of Valhalla they do."

Idon'tbelieveyouIdon'tbelieveyouIdon'tbelieveyou, Nick thought. They're not bad. Frigga didn't use me. I volunteered. Nick remembered her tears, remembered his desire to help her, and was almost completely sure he had done it all on his own. Almost.

Nick stared at the green-eyed god, knowing he shouldn't trust Loki but unable to ignore everything he said. Loki looked back as if he weren't the least bit interested in whether Nick believed him or not. "Will you tell me how to do it?" Nick said finally.

"Of course," said Loki.

"Why would you do that?" asked Nick as a feather of caution tickled the back of his neck.

"Because I don't want anything from you."

"You want my cards," countered Nick.

"Not anymore," Loki replied.

"You've been trying to take them since I got here," Nick accused.

"Sure," Loki admitted. "Angerbode, my wife, foretold that the path to my capture was written in a Sun Warrior's cards. That never bothered me much since we're a bit short on Sun Warrior's around here, as you probably noticed. But when you showed up, I figured I'd better get ahold of your cards or you. Of course, when I found you in the snow, most of your cards were blank, I couldn't read the ones that weren't, and they stung like angry bees. And you," he laughed, "you're harder to catch than a scared rabbit."

Loki gave a half-hearted tug on the chain. "It doesn't matter now. I'm caught. So," he sighed. "I don't really care about you or your cards anymore." He cocked his head at Nick. "Unless they say something else about me?"

Nick hadn't seen anything else about Loki in the cards and just enough caution, or fear, crept up in him that he wasn't about to get the cards out in front of the Trickster now. "No," he said. "The net was it."

Loki raised an eyebrow. "That was the only one? That hardly seems like enough to set One-Eye after me."

"Well, Baldur's card too," said Nick, not wanting to lie even to the old Trickster himself. "It said you were the one who tricked the blind man into throwing the mistletoe spear."

Loki nodded as if satisfied. "That makes more sense. Seemed like a good plan too. I didn't want to do that you know," Loki added quickly, apparently seeing the look that flashed across Nick's face at the mention of a "plan."

"But you did."

Loki shrugged, clinking his chain. "The fates of the giants and the gods are already woven. We must fight at Ragnarok. This was just part of that war, a war the gods fight as well as us." He looked again at Nick. "A war you are not a part of."

"If I'm not part of the war then tell me how to get back."

"It's simple. Do you still have your card, the one with your picture on it?"

Nick was startled that Loki knew about it. Then he remembered that he'd shown it to the fake King Thrym. Nick nodded.

"Burn it," said Loki. "When you do, you'll find yourself back in your land."

"That seems awfully easy," said Nick skeptically.

"It is." Loki stared right through Nick. "Odin should have told you days ago."

"How can that be?" asked Nick quietly.

"The card holds the magic that brought you here. When the card is destroyed, the magic will be released and you'll return to wherever it is you came from."

"Just burn the card," Nick said, not quite believing.

"And you'll be home."

"I could have done that any time," Nick said, half to himself.

"And spared yourself an awful lot of grief," Loki agreed.

A small fire suddenly sprang up between Nick and Loki. Nick jumped a little, startled by the pale orange flame that wasn't much bigger than a burner on a stove. Nick couldn't see what was burning. He looked at Loki for an explanation. Loki hadn't moved. He just sat there with the same smooth, calm look Nick remembered from the banquet hall.

"Go home, Sun Warrior," he said. "Burn the card."

Nick looked back at the small flame. "Odin said to wait," Nick said.

Loki scoffed. "Odin will tell you to wait until he runs out of errands for you. But what has old One-Eye ever done for you? Nothing. If he was doing what was best for you, he would have sent you home days ago, right after you got here."

Nick felt the fire's welcome heat on his face. Without thinking, he held out his hands to warm them.

"This land of cold and snow is not for you, Sun Warrior. Go home. Be warm again."

That got to Nick. He didn't belong here. He didn't belong in the snow and ice, and he certainly didn't belong in a land of hungry giants and horse-sized wolves. He felt like he hadn't been warm for days. He was tired and cold and he missed his parents more than ever. And all he had to do to see them again and be rid of this place was throw his Adventure Card into the fire.

"You just have to put it in," said Loki softly. "Then all this will be done."

Nick reached under his cloak for the card. Then he hesitated, instead crossing his arms and rubbing them, trying to keep warm while he thought.

His right hand touched the armring. And Nick realized what he had to do.

"I can't go," he said quietly.

"Sure you can," said Loki.

"I can't," repeated Nick. "I have something to do first."

"You've done enough for old One-Eye already." He rattled his chain. "How much more can you do?"

"It's not for him," replied Nick.

Loki's eyes narrowed. His eyes were like green lasers boring in on Nick. He stared at Nick's arm before his eyes lightened.

"Oh," Loki said. "The armring. That's simple enough. Take it with you."

"I can't. It's not mine."

"Baldur gave it to you, didn't he?"

"Yes."

"He's your friend?"

"Yes."

"Your friend gave it to you because he wants you to be safe, didn't he?"

"Yes," Nick reluctantly agreed again.

Loki shook his head. "It sounds like he's the one person who actually did something for you." Loki paused. "There are dangers in your world too, aren't there Sun Warrior?"

"Yes."

"You can be hurt or killed there, yes?"

The son of an astronaut was very aware of that possibility. "Yes."

"Not if you wear the armring," Loki whispered intently. "If you wear the armring, you'll be safe. You'll never have to worry about being hurt by anything or anyone." Loki's green eyes bored in on Nick. "You'll never have to fear wolves again."

Loki's final sentence hit Nick like a smack. It reminded Nick of the last thing Baldur had told him in Niffleheim. Suddenly, Nick laughed. Loki raised an eyebrow, questioning.

"I don't need the armring," said Nick. He leaned toward the god of mischief and looked him straight in the eye.

"I walked past the wolf without it."

Loki's eyes widened and in that moment, Nick saw the hunger, the green intensity with which Loki wanted him to burn the Adventure Card. Then he saw that intensity turn to rage.

Loki screamed. The small fire shot into the air. Nick leapt back, unsure whether he'd gotten out of the way or the armring had protected him. Loki strained against his chain. It sank deep into his chest, but it held.

The ground began to shake. The fire disappeared as Loki's eyes widened and flashed with panic. Nick scrambled to his feet and whirled to look behind him. Trees buckled and snapped and waved across the river, like tall grass bending before a wind Nick couldn't feel.

Odin was returning.

Nick turned back to Loki, who now had a calm, resigned look on his face. As the angry steps of the All Father pounded towards them, the god of mischief shook his head. "Almost," he said. "Almost." He gave Nick a wry smile. "Farewell, Sun Warrior. I don't think we'll meet again. Unless you plan to fight at Ragnarok?" Loki looked almost hopeful at the last question.

Nick shook his head quickly. "Pity," said Loki.

But that raised one last question that had bothered Nick since this all began. "Why?" he asked. "Odin lets you come to Valhalla with the gods. Why will you fight with the giants at Ragnarok?"

Loki smiled his half-smirking smile. "I have little choice."

"Why?"

"Because the giants will set me free."

With that Odin plowed into the river, his eye still blazing with unquenched rage. He walked straight over to Loki, flicked the chain from around the tree and flung the mischievous god over his shoulder like a sack. As he tramped away, he called over his shoulder, "I've sent Sleipnir back to you. He'll take you to Valhalla. Wait for me there." Then he disappeared with Loki into the woods.

Nick looked over at Hermod, who snored softly in the grass. Then he sat back down to wait for Sleipnir. It was getting dark. Hermod was asleep, and Odin was gone, leaving him alone at the edge of the forest.

Nick realized that he was not the least bit afraid.

Chapter 18

Nick stood on the shore of a gray sea. White-capped waves broke on the beach, crashing relentlessly in front of him. Nick shrugged deeper into his black furs to shield his neck against the wind blowing down from the snowy mountain peaks behind him. He shuddered, both from the cold and from why he stood there.

He was waiting for Baldur's funeral. Hermod and Sleipnir waited with him.

A ship lay beached on the shore before him, a ship that was easily the largest Nick had ever seen (and growing up in Florida, he'd seen a lot.) Enormous planks of dark wood curved from front to back and a black sail snapped lightly in the wind. At the front of the ship, a roaring dragon's head, complete with a forked tongue, rose well above Nick, quivering with each breaking wave as if it was eager to leap into the sea. At the back, a barbed tail curled and twisted just as high. *Hringham* the ship was called. It was Baldur's ship. And like Nick, it was waiting for Baldur.

Nick shuddered again as he stared at the pile of oil-soaked logs and branches stacked high on the ship's deck. He rubbed his eyes, as much to hide the sight of the funeral ship as to rub away fatigue. He was exhausted. Sleipnir had brought Nick (and a still groggy Hermod) back to Valhalla late last night, only a few hours earlier. There they'd been told by one of the battling heroes that the gods had left to prepare for Baldur's funeral and that Odin wanted the two of them and Sleipnir to be there. So, without a rest or a change or a sleep, and with only a quick mouthful of warm stew and bread, they'd traveled to the sea, and to Baldur's ship. Being Odin's eight-legged Wonder Horse and all, Sleipnir got them there before anyone else had arrived.

"Where are they, Hermod?" asked Nick, hunching down a little farther into his furs. Sleipnir considerately shuffled behind him to block the wind.

"Most are on their way," said Hermod. "A few are getting things ready."

Nick couldn't take his eyes off the massive, rocking dragon ship. "What are they going to do?" he asked quietly.

"The gods will come. They'll bring Baldur's body. They'll put it on the boat. We'll set fire to the boat and sing as it burns. Then we'll feast in his honor and tell tales of his bravery long into the night."

"A feast?" asked Nick. "You make it sound happy."

Hermod cocked his head at Nick. "Usually it is. Usually, it means we have another hero to fight with us at Ragnarok."

"But not this time," said Nick matter-of-factly.

Clip——clop, stamped Sleipnir half-heartedly.

"We'll miss him," said Hermod and, uncharacteristically for him, said no more.

Nick missed him too. He missed him terribly. He bowed his head as he realized he'd have to get used to it.

The call of a horn broke over the beach. Nick started around as the single, clear note echoed from the mountains. A line of people filed down the mountain road from Valhalla. But, as Nick has said about many things in the Norse lands, it was like no line of people he'd ever seen.

Odin strode at the front, a cape of white fur billowing behind him, his spear in one hand, his shield in the other. His single eye blazed as brightly as his eye patch was dark. His black crows, Hugin and Munin, rode on each shoulder but, for once, they stared straight ahead with no whispering. His wolves, Freki and Geri, loped along on either side of him, tails curled up, noses in the air, at full attention.

The Valkyrior marched with Odin as his honor guard. Though the sky was gray, the women's helmets shone like winged suns. The steel of their shields and spear heads glinted and their white robes shimmered so that they seemed like a shining white and gold and silver barrier surrounding Odin as he walked.

Walking next to Odin, among the riot of crows and wolves and warrior women, was Frigga. Walking, though, was the wrong word. She seemed to glide amidst the jostle of spears and paws and feathers, smooth and terribly still. She stood so straight she towered above the Valkyrior and the hair of her long golden braids was so bright it seemed to outshine their helmets. But as beautiful and graceful as she was, what grabbed

Nick's attention was the expression on her face, an expression of sadness that didn't look like it would go away. Ever.

Together, they all descended the mountain and spread out on the beach so that they started to surround the back of the dragon ship. As they gathered around him, Nick realized what was unusual about the company. They were utterly silent. Not a single person (or crow) spoke. They all just filed around Nick and Hermod and Sleipnir, Odin and Frigga taking a place on either side of them. And they waited.

When the Valkyrior (who seemed much taller when they were standing right next to him) had passed, Nick saw still more people making their way down the mountain. A blond man in a green shirt rode in a great chariot. Rather than horses though, the chariot was pulled by an enormous boar. "That's Frey," whispered Hermod.

"Is Frey the man or the pig?" asked Nick.

"The man, of course," said Hermod. "He's a god and that's Gullinbursti, his boar."

Nick's pocket began to buzz. He knew without looking that he now had a Frey card. But he didn't need to see it. He was watching the real thing.

"Gullinbursti," he whispered. And his pocket buzzed.

"That's his twin sister Freya, behind him," continued Hermod. "The most beautiful woman in Asgard."

Hermod's sigh told Nick there was a story there but the sight of Freya drove questions of it from his mind. She rode a chariot pulled by two great panthers. Her long blond hair flowed free behind her, blowing in the wind along with her billowing light blue dress. Nick had to agree with Hermod. She was beautiful. "Freya," Nick whispered. His pocket buzzed.

The cats, taller than Nick, silently padded past him, staring at him hungrily with large green eyes, and pulled Freya to their place at the end of the slowly growing line. On a hunch, Nick whispered, "Freya's cats." His pocket buzzed again.

Then, to Nick's surprise, Heimdall rode down, his red beard bouncing with the strides of his gigantic horse. His hand rested on the Giallar Horn at his side and as he passed Nick, he winked. The talkative Watchman of the Gods didn't say a word and reined his horse in next to Freya. Nick wanted to talk to Heimdall but took the hint from everyone else and kept quiet, except to whisper under his breath "Heimdall. The Giallar Horn." His pocket buzzed. And buzzed again.

Everyone around him turned and looked back up the mountain, so Nick did too. He gasped.

Giants were coming.

Towering, blue giants with bald heads and white beards. Dark-haired giants in brown jerkins carrying thick brown clubs in great dark hands. Monstrous giants with flaming red hair, pointed beards, and red swords.

"Odin's Beard," whispered Hermod to Nick. "All three tribes. Frost, Mountain, and Fire. I'd never have believed it."

"Believe it," rumbled Odin. Nick and Hermod started and looked up at him. "My son was well-loved." He stared at the approaching giants. "And quit mentioning my beard."

This was the only chance Nick had had to talk to Odin so he grabbed it. "Mr. Odin," said Nick. "Loki said you know how to send me home."

Odin tore his gaze away from the giants to stare at Nick. His eye blazed. "Don't mention that name to me now!" he growled. Nick backed up a step but held the All-Father's eye. Odin seemed to see Nick again and said, "I don't know how or I'd have done it long ago. There will be time to learn how to send you home." He looked back up the mountain. "After we remember my son."

A little shaken at Odin's anger and not sure he liked the god's answer, Nick looked back to the giants. A familiar figure walked at their head, a giant tall and wide (even for them), with a thick white beard and carrying a shining silver ax. Nick knew him at once.

"King Thrym," Nick whispered. His pocket buzzed.

The King of the Frost Giants strode directly up to Odin. He nodded his head, which should not in any way be mistaken for a bow, and said, "The giants wept for Baldur too. Ragnarok comes not this day."

Odin nodded and indicated a side. King Thrym guided his giants down next to Heimdall, whose hands twitched so severely on his horn that Nick thought for sure he'd break it. The Giant King stared at Nick as he passed, a stare Nick had grown used to from Norsemen (and Norse gods and giants) who had never seen a Sun Warrior before. As the Giant King's blue eyes assessed Nick, Nick knew immediately that he'd never seen them before, that he was meeting King Thrym for the first time. The expression on King Thrym's face said the same.

The giants took long moments to pass. But when they'd gone, one more man still came down the mountain.

Everyone Nick had met here, whether god or giant or hero or monster, was huge. This man seemed larger still. His hair was such a golden blond it was almost yellow and it hung loose around his massive shoulders. He wore a leather shirt with the sleeves cut away to free his enormously muscled arms. He wore a broad leather belt with a silver buckle and a pair of gloves that looked as though they were made of leather and steel. He wore high boots and though he seemed large as a tree to Nick, he moved quickly and lightly down the mountain. Any question Nick had about the identity of this man was answered by what was attached to the man's belt, bouncing next to his thigh.

A giant hammer.

"Thor," said Nick. Buzz.

"Yes," replied Hermod, thinking Nick was talking to him.

The god of thunder strode straight down the mountain towards Odin. Then Nick realized Thor wasn't looking at Odin. Thor was looking at him.

Nick's heart beat like Thor's hammer as the god of thunder walked up to him, then bent down on one knee. His head still towered above Nick's and he stared at Nick with blue, almost violet, eyes.

"You are the Sun Warrior," he said in an impossibly deep voice that sounded, well, like thunder.

"Yes," said Nick in a small voice.

"Are you the one who tried to save my brother?"

Nick felt a sudden rush of heat to his eyes. He couldn't speak for a moment because he was afraid he would cry and the last thing he wanted to do was blubber in front of the god of thunder. He cleared his throat. He cleared it again. Then he said, "Yes."

Thor put a gloved hand on Nick's shoulder. "Well done," he said. He gave Nick's shoulder a slight squeeze of thanks and stood.

Thor nodded to Odin, who clapped one hand fondly on his son's shoulder and guided him to the other side (which Nick noticed was the side farthest from the giants). With that Thor put a finger to his lips and whistled.

Two rows of yellow horses trotted down the mountain. Their manes and tails were long and pale, almost white, and hung far down their sides. The same pale hair hung from their forelegs, dancing as they high-stepped through the snow. The horses were hooked to a long, four-wheeled cart but there was no driver. The cart was flat and made of dark wood with large, rough, solid wooden wheels. On it rested a long table or pedestal, draped with a white cloth. On that pedestal lay Baldur.

No one moved as the horses pulled Baldur's cart down the mountain. Nick watched silently with everyone else as the team of pale horses brought the cart to rest in front of Odin. Baldur looked the same to Nick, like he was sleeping. He lay on his back, his head resting on a shield, like a pillow. Both hands were wrapped around the hilt of a sword that lay on his chest. He wore a shining steel breastplate, armor that he'd never needed, except once, when he was alive.

Three giants walked to the cart, one blue, one red, one brown. They placed a spear, a sword, and a club in the cart and returned to their place in line. Next, Heimdall walked up. He placed a large drinking horn on the cart next to Baldur's hand. He seemed to think better of it, picked up the horn, raised it to Baldur, and took a long drink. With a wipe of his beard, he tucked the horn under Baldur's arm and walked back to the line.

"What are they doing?" Nick whispered to Hermod.

"Giving him gifts to take with him," he whispered back.

"Where?" Nick asked.

Hermod nodded at the ship. Nick shuddered.

Frey, and then Freya, visited the cart but he couldn't see what either of them put there. Nick ducked his head as Frigga went next, not wanting to see the raw grief on her face as she said good-bye to her son. He kept his head down and sensed rather than saw Thor, and then Odin, go to the cart and return. And then he felt the weight of the stares of gods and giants.

"Nick," whispered Hermod. "Go."

Nick looked up, startled, not realizing he was expected to take a turn too. "But I don't have anything to give him," Nick whispered back.

Hermod's eyes were kind. "Then wish him a good journey."

Nick flashed a quick look up and down the line. Everyone was looking back. Nick raised his chin and started toward the cart, still not sure what exactly he was supposed to do.

It wasn't until much later (when I brought it up to him in fact), that Nick realized how very different this was for him. Remember, this was the same boy who wouldn't walk to a chalkboard in front of a class of sixth graders because he might not know an answer to a math problem. Now he was walking, with barely a flutter, in front of gods and giants and boars and panthers and crows and wolves (and did we mention GODS and GIANTS!) to a funeral cart with no idea what he'd do once he got there. ("It's amazing how different it is walking past someone when you know they're not going to eat you," he explained to me.)

Nick strode up to the cart. When he got there though, it was too tall—Nick couldn't reach Baldur. He couldn't even see him. So he did what any eleven-year-old boy would do in that situation. He climbed up.

Nick wasn't sure if it was a breach of Norse god funeral etiquette but grabbed the top of one of the wooden wheels and clambered into the cart. As he threw one leg over the edge, his black fur cloak snagged on a jagged splinter, catching him. He pulled and tugged, which just drove the splinter in farther. A little embarrassed now, he grunted and jerked as hard as he could. Abruptly, the clasp that fastened the cloak around his neck broke, sending Nick tumbling into the bottom of the cart, his cloak still draped over its side.

Nick reached up onto the pedestal and scrambled to his feet. The pedestal gave a little bit, and Nick realized that his hand was not grabbing the pedestal but Baldur's arm. Instinctively, he jerked his hand back. But then he looked down and saw not a ghoul or a goblin or a skeleton but Baldur. Just Baldur, who by some magic appeared just as he did when he first fell to the mistletoe spear. His red hair was neatly arranged around his shoulders, his hands were wrapped around the pommel of his sword, and his face was relaxed and calm, as if he were sleeping.

Nick had already cried for his friend. Now, he just missed him. He placed one hand on Baldur's. "I'm sorry," he said. "We almost did it. Everyone cried. Everyone but Loki. We, I, just didn't figure out it was him in time. I'm sorry."

Nick smiled a little. "But Odin got him. You should have seen him, changing from a fish to a man, both of them choking and red. Odin took him away somewhere so I don't think Loki will be able to do anything to anyone again." He patted Baldur's hand one more time. "Good journey, Baldur. Thanks." For everything.

Nick squeezed Baldur's hand one last time and turned to climb back off the cart.

Everyone was staring at him. He kind of expected that but more than staring, some were pointing and whispering. The giants especially.

Nick didn't think people, particularly the giant kind, would care that he'd climbed into the cart or that he'd talked to Baldur. Then he noticed that several of the giants were pointing at him and then pointing at their arms. Nick's stomach flipped. He looked down.

The armring glinted on his arm for all to see.

Since he had been completely focused on getting to Baldur (and since no one was trying to kill him), Nick had momentarily forgotten about it. He realized that it had been visible since his cloak had torn off, its red stone shimmering from atop Baldur's funeral cart.

The giants were becoming more and more agitated, pointing and speaking louder and louder in their guttural tongue. He heard a few yells and the crash of a club on a shield.

The commotion was irritating the gods. Odin was facing the giants, his spear and shield held upright now in each arm. Thor's hammer had appeared in his hand. The Valkyrior lowered their spears. Heimdall fingered his horn as if he were thinking about sounding it. Only Frigga stared at Nick, her arms crossed, her lips pressed together in what was almost a frown. Her eyebrows were raised in an unspoken question to him. She didn't move, though the chaos around her grew.

It looked to Nick like Ragnarok might start right here and now. And he knew, without thinking, what he must do.

Nick turned back to Baldur and slipped off the armring. He pulled one of Baldur's hands off his sword hilt and slid it up his friend's arm, past his elbow. As before, it adjusted to Baldur's size. Nick clasped Baldur's cold hand with both of his.

"You're the most worthy warrior I ever met," Nick said. "I give it to you."

Nick felt regret at giving up the armring, but only for a moment. As he looked down at the white metal, he knew that it was, without question, the best thing he'd ever owned and that he'd never have anything like it ever again. He also knew it wasn't his, that he should give it back, and that it should stay here, in Asgard. He didn't need it anymore. Not really. Loki wasn't trying to kill him. And he wasn't afraid.

No, Nick knew it was time to give the armring up (although he had to admit, he was a little tempted to take it home and go out for the football team). He also knew he'd never be able to pick one person out of that squabbling bunch that was worthy of it. So he gave it to the one person he knew was. Let them figure out what to do with it now, he thought.

With one last pat of Baldur's arm, Nick turned and threw a leg over the side of the cart. He was wrung out and wanted, more than ever, to go home.

Then there was a ragged breath like someone bursting from the deep end of a swimming pool. Nick froze, not wanting to turn around.

"Still agitating them, I see," said a voice from the cart. "What do you have against giants, lad?"

Not believing, Nick turned around. Baldur was sitting up in the cart, long red hair streaming around his shoulders, a smile visible even through his thick beard.

"Nothing," said Nick. "They seem to have something against me."

Then Nick flung himself into Baldur's arms and squeezed as hard as he could.

Chapter 19

A riot of shouts erupted around Nick and Baldur and it was some time before Nick could actually speak to him. Gods rushed the cart and before Nick knew what was happening, he was buried under a flurry of hugs, kisses, backslaps, and bellows (and at least one face licking although from wolf, horse, or boar he couldn't tell). In it all, he heard Thor's thunderous shout, Odin's harsh cackle, and a sound so beautiful and pure it sounded like bells.

It was Frigga's laugh.

Eventually, the push lessened and Nick was able to catch his breath. "What happened?" rumbled Thor.

"Young Snow brought me back," replied Baldur with a smile.

"We see that," said Thor. "How?"

"The armring," said Baldur. "It stays with the wearer's spirit. When Nick gave it to my body, it brought my spirit back."

"But you always had the armring," said Thor. "Why didn't you just bring yourself back?"

Baldur shook his head. "My body didn't have it—my spirit did. If I'd used it in Niffleheim, it would have brought my body to me there, instead of bringing my spirit back here."

Thor looked at Nick for the first time. "So you knew this all along? Why didn't you do it a few days ago?"

"I didn't know," said Nick quietly.

"You didn't know?" asked Thor incredulously. "Then why'd you do it?"

"Because Baldur told me to give the armring to the most worthy warrior I could find," said Nick. "That's him." Baldur smiled and actually blushed a little. "And because it didn't belong to me, no matter what Loki said."

"What did Loki say?" asked Baldur quickly.

"He told me to take it home with me, that it would protect me from things there just as well as it did here."

"Why would Loki say that?" asked Hermod.

"Because Loki wanted to send Nick home with the armring," Baldur replied.

Odin caught on immediately. "Because if the armring is in Fl . . . What's it called, Sun Warrior?"

"Florida."

"Florida," Odin said slowly as if he had trouble saying the sunny word. "If the armring is in Florida with the Sun Warrior, it can't be with us at Ragnarok."

"And if it isn't here with us at Ragnarok, the giants could win," said Baldur.

"Looks like the giants have figured that out," said Thor, pointing behind them to where the giants had stood.

They were gone. Not a single giant remained on the shore.

"They must have known about Loki's plot," Thor continued. "When they saw Baldur rise, they knew it had failed."

Suddenly, there was a deep rumble beneath their feet. Nick's legs trembled. He thought it was just him until he saw everyone else grabbing the cart for support. The earth was shaking.

A moment later it stopped and Odin rasped in laughter. "Looks like Loki has figured it out too." They all looked questioningly at Odin. "I bound him under the earth at the very roots of Ygdrasill," Odin explained proudly. "I put a snake above him to drip venom on his head every minute for all eternity. His wife was trying to catch the venom in a cup when I left but if she misses, or if he gets disturbing news, the earth is going to shake." He looked at his feet and gave a wolfish grin. "I'd bet he just found out what happened to his plan."

Nick shuddered at that. Then he remembered why Loki said he would side with the giants at Ragnarok: *Because they will release me.*

"So that's what this is about? Why he killed Baldur in the first place? Why he tried to keep us from bringing him back?" asked Nick. "To gain an advantage at Ragnarok?"

"Yes," Baldur nodded. "And sending you back with the armring would have done the trick just as well."

The smile died on Nick's face. Baldur saw it. "What?"

"Nothing," said Nick quickly. "Well, we'll just . . . we still have to figure out how to send me home." He looked at Odin. "Do you know how?"

Odin gazed seriously at Nick. "No, Sun Warrior," he said. "I don't."

"I didn't think so," said Nick, dropping his eyes to hide his disappointment.

"How did Loki think you were going to get home?" asked Hermod.

"He told me how." Nick looked at Odin. "He said you knew too."

"If I knew, I would have told you," said Odin gruffly.

"He said you just weren't telling me. Because you wanted me to do things for you. Things you didn't want your own men to do." Before Nick could stop himself, he glanced at Baldur.

Odin stared at Nick, his eyebrow furrowed in a scowl. "People have called me many things, Sun Warrior. A coward who hides behind children is not one of them. If I had known your way home, I would have set you on it the moment we met."

Nick felt the gods all nodding around him. Baldur and Hermod each put a hand on his shoulder. Now, surrounded by them and feeling their friendship and affection, he couldn't believe he'd listened to Loki. But, as I told you before, it's much different repeating the words Loki said (or reading them on a page) than it is hearing them directly from the Trickster himself.

"Wait," said Baldur suddenly. "What did he tell you to do?"

Nick cocked his head. "Throw my Adventure Card into the fire."

"Adventure Card?" asked Baldur.

"The red one, with my picture on it," said Nick. "He said its magic is what brought me here and that if it's destroyed, the magic will be released and send me home."

Baldur thought for a minute. The other gods watched him. "It must be true," he said finally.

"Why?" asked Thor.

"Because Loki really wanted to get rid of Nick and the armring. The best thing that could have happened for him was if Nick found his way home still wearing the armring." Baldur thought a moment more. "The Trickster must have been telling the truth on this. It's the only way his plan would have worked."

"The best lies are based on truth," Hermod said helpfully. "Like this one time when I took a jar of honey Father was using to make . . ."

"HERMOD!" a chorus of gods yelled.

"Sorry," Hermod said, bowing his head sheepishly. "I mean, I agree."

"Well, that's it then," said Odin. "We'll send the Sun Warrior home. Just as soon as we feast in his honor. He's brought home my son!" he yelled raising his shield.

The other gods yelled in raucous agreement.

"As long as it's hot," Baldur smiled at Nick. "I just can't stand anymore cold chicken."

Nick thought he hid how he felt, but apparently he didn't do it very well. "What is it, lad?" asked Baldur.

"I'm sorry, I'd like to but . . ." his voice caught. He leaned forward and spoke very quietly. "It's just that I've been gone a very long time."

"Of course you have, lad," said Baldur immediately. "We were just thinking of ourselves." Baldur raised his hand to the crowd. "The Sun Warrior's home has been too long without his protection. We must send him back now. Then our feast will celebrate his great deeds." Because there was still going to be a feast, the gods cheered again.

Baldur returned to Nick. "Though I must admit I was looking forward to sharing a meal with you." He smiled. "Our last one didn't go so well."

Nick, being the polite boy that he was, started to offer to stay through the feast. "No, no," said Baldur, waving a hand. "You've been gone long enough. Let's get you home."

"Thanks," said Nick. He'd never meant that word more.

Nick and Baldur sat on a small dune near the dragon ship, waiting for the others who wanted to see Nick off. Nick was glad to finally have a moment to talk to his friend.

"So you think all I have to do is burn the Adventure Card?" asked Nick.

"It makes sense," said Baldur, nodding. "Loki had to get rid of you for his plan to work. And we know the magic in the card is what brought you here. That's got to be the way to undo it."

Nick remembered all the dangers—the giants, the wolves, the underworld—and shook his head. "All those times I was almost killed. A little fire and I could have gone home any-time. Geez, if I'd thrown it into that fire you made for me after you saved me from the giants, I could have avoided all of it."

"True," said Baldur, nodding slowly. "But think what would have happened if you had left right away. I'd have been killed but no one would have brought me back. The armring would be in Niffleheim but I'd have no one to give it to. Worst of all, Loki would still be free because no one would have discovered his plot or found where he was hiding." Baldur shook his head. "Maybe things would have been the same for you if you'd left, but they would have been much different here." Baldur smiled. "Personally, I'm glad you stayed."

The two sat for a moment, thinking. "No, things would have been different for me too," said Nick finally. "If I'd re-turned right away, I'd never have ridden a horse. I'd never have met gods or seen Valhalla. I'd never have met my second-best friend."

Baldur raised an eyebrow. Nick shrugged, "Chris has you by a few years." They both smiled.

"But I think the most important thing," Nick continued, "is that if I'd returned in the clearing, at the very beginning, before all this happened, I never would have walked past the wolf."

Baldur nodded and studied Nick for a moment. "It would have been easier for you if you'd been sent back right away," agreed Baldur finally. "And I have no doubt that the people of your land are brave and strong. But if you had been sent back then, I do not think you would have become the man you now are. Sun Warrior."

"Thanks," was all Nick could say.

The two sat a moment longer, shoulders touching, in the silence of deep friendship. Eventually, Baldur pointed. Nick saw a group, including an eight-legged horse, making its way up the beach towards them.

"There are some people who want to say good-bye," said Baldur putting his hand on Nick's shoulder. "Then we'll send you on your way."

The group turned out to be Hermod and Sleipnir along with Thor, Odin, and Frigga. All of them (the non-horses anyway) were grinning.

"You saved us from a storm, Sun Warrior," rasped Odin. "And you gave up a fair bit to do it. Not many would have given up the armring even knowing it would bring Baldur back and you did it without knowing just because you thought it was right." It took Nick a moment to follow that but then he got it.

"You gave it up without a thought of reward," rumbled Thor, and took a knee in front of Nick. "So we want to give you one."

"No, you don't have to do that . . ." started Nick (those good manners again).

"Of course we don't," snapped Odin with a wolfish grin, his one eye twinkling. "But we're going to. And unless you have another armring in your pocket, I don't think you can stop us."

"Okay," smiled Nick.

Thor held out one hand, spreading his fingers wide so Nick could see the leather and iron glove he wore. "These are magic gauntlets," the Thunderer said. "The Night Elves made them for me so I could swing this," he indicated the giant hammer swinging from the loop on his belt. He pulled a smaller pair of gloves out of his belt and held them out to Nick. "This is the pair from when I was a child. They're not powerful enough to let you swing my hammer but I think you'll find they give you strength enough." He slapped Nick lightly on the shoulder (which almost knocked him over) as Nick took the gloves and put them on. "I won't forget what you did for my brother," Thor said, and stepped back.

Nick didn't feel anything different as he flexed his fingers but had little time to think about it as Odin moved in front of him. Hugin and Munin cackled from the old god's shoulders as the All Father towered above Nick, hands on hips. "My crows have taken a liking to you, Sun Warrior. So my gift to you is that when you return to your land, this Florida, one time, and one time only, you'll be able to understand the speech of birds. Use it only when you must." He held out one great hand. "I'd never have caught that Trickster without you." Nick took the hand and, whether because of the gloves or extreme control by Odin, it wasn't crushed by the god.

Frigga knelt then in front of Nick, her golden braids trailing the ground. Finally, finally after all these days, she smiled. Now do you remember that backpack full of bricks I've told you about, the one Nick felt like he had been carrying all this time? At that moment, when Frigga really and truly smiled, it finally dropped from Nick's shoulders.

When Frigga held out her arms, Nick went to her and hugged her. "Thank you, Sun Warrior," she said and squeezed him a little tighter.

Nick squeezed her back. As he let go, she quickly placed a chain around his neck, then folded his cloak around it. If he'd grown up in the north, it would've reminded Nick of a mom tucking a scarf into his winter coat. He reached up for it but Frigga grabbed his hand and patted it. "Don't look," she whispered in his ear. "Leave it under your cloak until you get home." She fastened his cloak shut in the front.

"What. . . ?"

"It was hidden in the armring," she said quietly. "No one else here knows about it, not Odin or Thor or even Baldur. It's the other part of its power." She paused. "The part that was meant for you."

Nick looked up at her in surprise but Frigga just put one finger on his lips and smiled. "Hush," she said. "And thank you."

As Frigga rose, Odin, Thor, and Baldur were watching the party growing around the dragon ship. "I have a couple of things to get ready," said Baldur. "It's my funeral after all. Come down when you're done." With a quick smile and a wave, Baldur headed for his ship. Frigga slipped one of her arms into Odin's and, along with Thor, followed Baldur down to the sea.

"Well," said Hermod, "I haven't heard of anything like this since the time Thor went to the giants and tried to drink the ocean and lift the Midgard Serpent and . . ." Hermod stopped on his own, mouth open. "Sorry," he said. "I keep doing that."

Now that he was about to leave him, Nick found he'd actually miss Hermod's stories. Sometimes anyway. He slapped the side of Hermod's big arm (a very Norse gesture) and grinned. "I can't think of a better way to pass the time. Especially in the dark on the way to the underworld."

Clip-CLOP-clip, stamped Sleipnir in half-hearted agreement.

Hermod grinned back. "Maybe next time you can show me those buffalo horns of yours."

"Buffalo wings, Hermod. Buffalo wings. And if you ever end up in Florida, I'll get you the spiciest batch."

"Great," said Hermod. "I can't wait to eat flying cow."

Nick started to correct him but saw the sparkle in Hermod's eye first. The two clasped arms. They'd stormed the gates of Niffleheim together. Nothing more needed to be said.

The same went for Sleipnir. The great horse nuzzled Nick's shoulder. Nick put one hand into that thick gold mane and rubbed behind one ear. "Thanks," said Nick.

Clip-CLAP-clip-clip, stamped Sleipnir.

Nick stamped too. He'd had enough of good-byes.

He was ready to go home.

The Norse were never ones to wait on a party and their gods were no exception. As Nick walked down to the sea, he heard the shouts and singing of a first class feast. He came up next to Baldur behind the dragon ship which was now surrounded by singing heroes, many of whom held torches for light as the sun set.

Baldur met Nick with a wink and a smile. Then he raised the horn at his side and sounded it. The clear tone echoed over the sea and the heroes fell silent.

Baldur raised his hands. "Brothers," he shouted.

"Hail," yelled the throng of heroes, raising their own torches in salute.

"I see you prepared my ship."

"Aye!" roared the throng.

"Turns out, I won't be needing it."

"Aye!" roared the heroes, even louder than before.

"But since you've ruined the finish with all this oil, we might as well use it to send our Sun Warrior off in proper Norse style!"

"Aye!"

Baldur raised his horn again. "To young Snow, our brother in arms, a hero of Asgard." He looked directly at Nick now.

"I know not where the Sun Warriors go but may his path bring him one day back to Valhalla."

"Sun Warrior! Sun Warrior! Sun Warrior!" the heroes roared with "Hail, Snow!" and Baldur grinned as he turned to Nick. "Give me your card, lad."

Nick, who'd been expecting it, pulled the Adventure Card out of his pocket. He waited as Baldur set down his horn and picked up a bow. He nocked an arrow and aimed for the ship. "Put the card over the point, lad," he said, holding the arrow steady.

Nick did as he was told, sliding the card over the large, pointed arrow head. It cut through the card easily.

With a smooth draw and release, Baldur sent the arrow, and the card, arcing onto the deck of the ship, where it hit the funeral bier so recently intended for him. While the arrow still quivered in the wood, Baldur lifted his bow over his head. "Hail, Sun Warrior!" he cried.

"Hail, Sun Warrior!" the heroes cried in return, and threw their torches up onto the ship's deck, their flames streaking in yellow arcs through the deepening darkness. Then all the heroes got behind the ship and pushed, slowly scraping it along the sand into the sea.

The dragon ship inched into the sea, its head bobbing now in the waves. With a final push, the heroes heaved the rest of the ship into the water just as a burst of wind caught its black sail, sending the ship jumping onto the waves and fanning the flames on the deck. Readied by the oil, the dragon's black neck and the stem of its dark tail burst into yellow flame, sending a shower of sparks towering into the air and scattering them across the black sail like lightning bugs. The dark cloth caught, and the black, almost invisible sail burst into a rectangle of fiery orange.

The heroes swayed, arms around each others shoulders, and sang as the rest of the ship caught fire. Accompanied by their loud (and slightly off-key) song, flaming timbers began to fall into the sea, sending up billows of smoke and steam. Just then, the wind shifted, coming around to blow in toward shore. Clouds of grey smoke and white steam rolled from the boat directly into Nick's face. He coughed a little and waved one hand but the smoke only grew thicker. He stepped to the side to try and get out of the cloud stream but the smoke just swirled thicker around him.

"Nick!" he heard Baldur call. He coughed harder now and took another step, reaching out for where Baldur had stood a moment before. His foot caught and he tumbled forward, waving his arms trying to catch himself on his friend. "Nick!" he heard Baldur yell again, louder this time. But Nick couldn't reach him.

The smoke surrounded Nick. He coughed and struggled as the cloud pressed down on him. Soon it became so thick he couldn't see at all and he coughed harder as it scratched his throat. He thrashed at the smoke, trying to get free but now he could feel it all over his skin, wrapping itself around him like a thick gray blanket.

"Nick!" boomed the voice. "We're late for . . . Sweet Blazes what have you done?!"

Nick recognized the expression before he recognized the voice. They both belonged to James Snow.

Nick scrambled up towards his dad but his feet kept getting caught in the gray blanket. His gray blanket. The blanket that usually lay on his bed. He reached up and pulled it down, hand over hand, over his head. It came off of him and his head popped up into a cloud of goose feathers. The first thing Nick saw was his father, standing straight and tall in the doorway, the doorway to his room, hands on his hips, his face looking like one of Thor's thunderclouds.

Nick didn't care a bit. "Dad!" he yelled as he scrambled to his feet. He shot across the room, and jumped in a swirl of feathers into his dad's arms. His dad was too shocked to do anything but catch him as Nick rattled "DadDadDad! I've been trying to get back but first Baldur died and then I had to go get him and no one knew how to send me back and I kept trying to come back but I just couldn't find the way but finally Baldur figured it out after he was dead and when he came back he told me we had to burn the card so we did . . ."

Nick felt his dad stiffen. James Snow loosened Nick's grip, pushed him away, and set Nick back on the ground. He put both hands on Nick's shoulders and stared at Nick. "Nick," he said in his quiet, space shuttle command voice. "What did you say?"

Nick was so happy he was stuttering a little but he raced on again, "I've been trying to get back. I'm sorry I was gone but I've been trying to get back but no one knew how."

James Snow's eyes were now very wide. "Nick," he said softly. "Slow down. Talk to me slowly."

Nick took a deep breath and said, "Pabbi, fyrirgefðu. Ég get ekki að því gert! Ég veit ekki . . ."

Now Nick's eyes widened. He finally heard it. He was speaking another language. And thinking in it.

Nick took another deep breath. He started again, in what he knew was English this time. "I've been trying to get back. But I couldn't find my way."

As his father studied him, Nick suddenly felt very hot. Then he realized he still wore his black furs and boots, which were covered with a sprinkling of white feathers. He followed his dad's eyes from his furs to his wreck of a room. When he felt the fingers tighten on his shoulders, Nick realized that his dad had never let go of him.

James Snow pulled Nick in again and now he squeezed Nick as tight as his son had squeezed him the moment before. "I can see you have something to tell me," he said. He squeezed again and then let Nick go. "We'll figure it out together."

Nick smiled, knowing it was true.

"But first, we'd better clean up this room. And quickly. Or your mother will kill us."

Of all the dangers Nick had recently faced, that was the most feared. And most welcome.

Epilogue

"So what was it?" I asked.

"What was what?" Nick asked back.

"What Frigga put around your neck," I replied.

"Oh," said Nick. "This." He pulled at a silver chain around his neck and flipped a white skeleton key out from under his shirt.

"Do you know what it is, Mr. Minion?" asked James Snow.

"No," I replied because at that time I had only guesses. "But I'd keep it close if I were you. And I wouldn't tell anyone about it."

James Snow didn't look happy with that answer and I couldn't really blame him. But I wasn't worried about that right then. Instead I asked, "What about the gloves? Have you tried them?"

The two grinned at each other and nodded.

"And?" I asked.

Nick reached under the couch and pulled out an aluminum baseball bat. It was bent in the shape of a U.

That surprised me. "You?" I asked Nick. Nick nodded. "Did you try them?" I asked Mr. Snow.

He nodded. "They don't fit." That did not surprise me.

"They're not meant for you," I said. "So what happened after Nick got back?"

"We didn't leave for Tampa on time, that's for sure," said Mr. Snow with another smile at his son. "Nick told me everything that had happened. I had a hard time believing him at first. I mean the story he told happened over weeks and he'd only been gone a few minutes. But he was wearing those furs and speaking that language. He can still speak it by the way."

I looked at Nick. He nodded.

"I called a friend of mine over at Gainesville, at the University of Florida. He put me in touch with a language professor. We had Nick say a few things. The guy recognized it as old Icelandic. He was pretty curious where Nick would have learned it."

"What did you tell him?"

"I told him I found it on the internet. On a video game," said Nick brightly, obviously proud of the fib.

"And?"

"He believed me."

"Nice."

"So," continued James Snow, "between the furs and the gloves and the key, it was hard not to believe him, no matter how incredible the story." Mr. Snow paused for a moment. "Plus, after a couple of days his mom and I both realized he was . . . different."

"How?" I asked, very interested.

"More confident. Braver."

"Beating the god of mischief will do that to a man," I replied. Nick beamed.

Mr. Snow nodded again. "It's obvious something happened. It's still just hard for me to believe that a card in a game could have done this."

I raised an eyebrow.

"You remember what I said, Mr. Minion," said Nick. "To bring me back, they burned my Adventure Card. So when I was home, the card was gone and I couldn't show my Dad."

"Is that all?" I asked. I reached into an inside pocket and pulled out an Adventure Card, the Nick Snow Adventure Card. "Would you like to see it?"

James Snow whipped an arm across Nick's chest like he had slammed on the brakes of his car. "Don't touch it, Nick," he said, his eyes wide.

"Don't worry, Dad," said Nick, his eyes wider.

I held it out for both to see. "Sweet Blazes, Nick," whispered Mr. Snow. "It is you."

"I know," said Nick quietly.

"What about the rest of your cards?" I asked.

Nick reached into his pocket and pulled out a worn deck of blue cards. "There're no blanks," he said, fanning them out. "Once I came back, you could see them all."

"That makes sense," I said. They looked a question at me. "There are no gods or giants trying to get the cards now. There is nothing to protect you from anymore." I hoped.

"What does it mean?" asked Mr. Snow. "How could this have happened?"

"I don't know," I replied, which was almost entirely true. "But I'll tell you when I find out."

"How are you going to do that?" asked Nick.

"There are others like you," I said and Nick's eyes almost glowed. "You're the first I've spoken to. I've learned of another, a girl in Texas named Anna Verde and I hear she likes to sing songs about very strange places. I'm going to talk to her next."

"Does she have a card too?" asked Nick.

"Of course," I replied.

"What does hers say?" he asked.

I replaced the Nick Snow Card in my pocket and pulled out the Anna Verde Adventure Card. I held it up for Nick (James Snow put his hand in front of Nick again to keep him from touching it and I can't say as I blame him) so he could see the picture of the dark-haired girl sitting cross-legged. She had head phones around her neck and was singing. Underneath the picture was written:

Anna Verde wished music could change her world. It would.

The Adventure card is the key. Brace yourself.

"That doesn't sound good," said James Snow.

"It worked out for me, Dad," said Nick.

"So far," replied Mr. Snow cautiously. Which showed he shared my misgivings about why Nick had been allowed to bring back what he did. And my curiosity about the white key around his neck. "You'll let us know what you hear?" he asked.

"Of course," I replied and stood.

"Any suggestions in the meantime?" Mr. Snow asked.

"Keep the story to yourself for now . . ."

"Don't worry about that," muttered Nick.

". . . and don't show anyone else what you brought back with you."

They each cocked their head to the side in the exact same way. It was easy to see that Nick Snow was his father's son.

"If I found you, others might too. And I'm not sure you'll want to meet all of them."

James Snow stood very straight, as if daring someone to enter his house against his will. Without looking at him, Nick Snow straightened right along with him. Like I said, he was his father's son.

"Thank you, Mr. Minion," said James Snow and held out his hand.

"Scrivener, please," I said as I shook it. "Nick," I reached out a hand to him. Nick took it with a grip stronger than one would expect of an eleven-year-old, a grip which had obviously been strengthened by grabbing the mane of an eight-legged horse very tightly. "I've not heard such a tale in a very long time, and I've heard more than you'd believe. You earned your name back there in Asgard. Well done, Sun Warrior."

"Thanks," said Nick and smiled.

"Tell us what you hear," said Mr. Snow again.

"You can be sure I will," I replied.

Then I left for Texas.

Look for the tale of Anna Verde
in the next Mytmatical Battles Adventure,
Sing the Giant's Song